ONE

It seemed like there was nothing outside the car, but noise and darkness. The rain fell from the night sky so hard and so heavy it hit the car park and bounced, before it washed away to join the growing lake around the overwhelmed drains. We were parked in the darkest, loneliest corner, well away from the green and white lights of the supermarket. It is open all night, but parked in the shadows, with the lights down, I doubt we would have drawn much attention on any night.

In the storm we were all but invisible. The headlights of customers and people with nowhere else to be rolled past in the distance, made vague and ethereal by the cascades.

My hands were still resting on the wheel, because I suddenly had no idea what else to do with them. My throat was dry, my tongue felt like sand paper, and my heart was jumping off my stomach and catching in my gullet. I glanced across to Penny. She was curled up on the passenger seat, toying with her bleached white hair, looking at me with sympathy in her eyes and mischief on her smile. She had two paper bags on her lap. A take out order from the Piri-Piri Hut. Her chicken breast sandwich was Diablo hot, with a side of slaw and a tall shake. Mine was marinated in mango and lemon, with a side of fries and a bottle of zero-cal soda.

She let her smile tweak. "This is fine."

"Sure?" I looked around. "People might think we are..." I let the words trail off.

"We might be." She grinned. "Anything is better than going home right now."

I grinned and tried not to look hurt. I guess I failed.

"I'm kidding." Penny said, after a few awkward moments. "I mean, if you ever try to do that with me and I happen to let you, it will be because I kind of like the idea, not because it's better than going home." She winced at her own words and put her head on the glass. "No. Wait. If I wanted that it would most definitely be better than going home and..."

"And that doesn't mean you want me to try tonight." I smiled and took my bag. "Do you want to talk about why you don't want to go home?"

"Honestly?" She started to unwrap her chicken sandwich. "No. I appreciate you asking, but I don't."

"Okay." I stared at the bag on my lap without eating anything.

"You don't do this very often do you?" Penny asked. "Meet strangers from the dating site?"

"Not often." I was all too aware of how awkward my smile looked. "I've been on there a year now and had maybe four dates."

"Four before me?" She flushed.

"No. Four dates total." I shifted back away from her, up against the side of the car. "Including this one." I shifted a little from her gaze. "From the dating site. Four times, with three people, for dates. Years ago, when I was nineteen or twenty I met loads of friends from chat rooms, social media, as friends. Some stayed friends. Some I lost after seeing them as more than friends. But... Then I got married and it all changed."

"Is that why, when I said I did not want to go home, you asked where I would want to be rather than suggesting a nice warm house?" Penny was careful about her tone. There was no suggestion I was asking the wrong questions. "That it feels like you are cheating taking somebody home?"

"It still feels like it is her home too." I admitted.

"Tell me what happened." Penny leaned over and put her hand on my knee. Not in a flirty way, not squeezing or tickling. Just emphasising her words. "Please."

"You mean was it my fault or hers?" I asked.

She nodded.

"Neither. We just fell out of love. We married at twenty four, we lasted nearly ten years. We were doing fine until she got a dream opportunity up in London. I tried to follow her, to spend time there and support her. She has a flat we were renting, and we were going to sell up here to buy her some time to take the chance, I took on extra work grading papers to cover the costs, and life just got hard. We got tired. We got stressed. We argued a bit. Then she started saying stuff she didn't mean. That she had no friends in London that she didn't meet through work, like it was my fault. That my family weren't her family. That I was in the way. It got real bad real slow for three months, then fell apart over a week." I stopped fooling myself that I would be able to eat, and put the fry back in the packet. My stomach thanked me. "I stopped trying to sell the house. I moved back, just for a while. For the six days I was down here, I rang her every day, trying to get some sign of life from her. But I got voice mail, and promises from her PA that she would be right back in touch. The seventh day, the Saturday, was our anniversary. We had always planned to be here. When she didn't show and I got the same lame excuse, something broke. I was already pretty low, and the idea I was toxic to her. The idea that she sounded so much happier on voice mail messages when she had not seen me than when we were face to face. It tore me apart and I don't even remember issuing the divorce paper."

"But she signed them?" Penny looked at me with those eyes full of sympathy again.

"Not at first." I had to look away from her. To watch the rain. "She rang me up to scream at me down the phone. To ask if I was kidding her. If I was making a sick joke. If I cared about her at all. She gave me both barrels and ripped out my spleen, before I asked when she last answered a call or saw me. Then... Then she stopped and couldn't. She just told me she thought we had been getting on okay the last few days. She was happier."

"Jesus." Penny whispered, which seemed a fair assessment. "She's a bitch."

"No." I said, quietly. "She isn't. She just didn't handle it very well. She shut me off. I never got to go and collect my stuff from London, she posted me some. We signed papers in a month. A week later she had a party with all those friends from her work that she had in London. One of them, a twenty three year old gym fanatic from Chelsea was her boyfriend in another few weeks. She was spending of most her time with him from the party, but only really considered him a boyfriend after another month or so." I smiled. "In her head she was writing this fairy tale. She was trying to make it so I was the monster, and she was the victim and all that jazz. Her friends back here were treating me like I was an ogre. They let me know I had been scum. So I went to try and fix things. Just to talk to her."

"Oh." Penny was shaking her head as she spoke with a mouth full of chicken sandwich. "No. No. Bad move. Poor silly boy."

"Yeah." I closed my eyes. "Stupid me. She thought I was there to fight and her boyfriend blocked me. Pretty much threatened to beat the crap out of me if I set foot in the flat. I am pretty sure I looked pathetic. Thing is, he is not a bad guy either, or at least not the villain. So I asked if he minded talking a while? If I couldn't tell her myself, could he try to understand?"

"Really?" Penny, was shaking her head.

"Really." I smiled. "And he wanted me away from the flat, so yeah, he let me buy him a pint and he gave me a few minutes to say what I had to say."

"Which was?" Penny looked relieved the story did not end with me hurting Jean, or the Police dragging me from her doorstep, while I wailed at the moon.

"That ten years of love did not end, just because she hurt me." I felt stupid saying it again. "No. Not that I was still in love with her, but that I never stopped loving her. That yeah, having my chance to say goodbye properly, to speak this over when I was supposed to collect the watercolours and the books from her flat hurt, and that receiving them by courier was a bit of a slap in the face, but not one I was going to resent. That she fobbed off my family."

"The whole 'you ain't my family' thing? Ouch! That could pretty easily be taken as bitch talk." Penny said, firmly. "You sure she wasn't..."

"She was just hurting." I said.

"Did he understand that?" She asked. "The boyfriend?"

"Kind of." I smiled weakly. "Not exactly what I said. But... He understood things looked different from where I was standing. I mean, he only really knew her after the divorce and all he could judge me by was the amount of hurt he saw her in. Crying and alone. As far as he was concerned I was the cold son of a bitch who never asked if she was okay. He was ready to thump the table and ask if I loved her so much, where I was when she was hurting? How hard was it to pick up a phone and check she was okay?" I paused. "But he had never seen her ring me. She asked her friends about me and she got gossip. She never picked up a phone. Never asked if I was okay. She probably thought I was ungrateful for not thanking her for the watercolours. I asked him what if I had carried on ringing her after the first few weeks. How long before he thought I was a stalker. How long before he thought he needed to call the Police, or to do a lot more than kick my arse. He stopped. He thought. He saw a little of it from my point of view."

"So?" Penny asked.

"So life isn't a fairy tale. It doesn't end with the twenty something gym bunny chasing her across an airport and declaring her love. We all have this story in our heads where we are the heroes. Right now you are telling a story in your head where I am the guy you really regret asking about this stuff on a date." I said.

"No." She shook her head. "Right now I am telling the story in my head where you are one of the nice people on the internet, who mean it when you say we can meet up as mates, and not worry too much if it doesn't feel like a date."

"Whatever. The point is, it is your story. In your head it is your story. You asked about this stuff, and I am answering. In my head, the story looks a little different. And for Jean, it looks different again. Seeing reasons you are the hero is easy. Seeing reasons the other person is the villain is easy. Seeing reasons you are a bitch, they are difficult." I felt the sadness in my smile. "I know I argued with her. I know things fell apart. I know I was the one who walked away. I know I hurt her."

"She needed you to be the bastard, because otherwise she has to ask what kind of a bitch doesn't notice her husband is not home for a week." Penny smiled. "Yeah. I can see that skews the point of view a bit more."

"That's one of the things she noticed." I nodded.

"What else?" She thought about it a while. "Why didn't you ring her, or call her, or make the effort to be there before?"

I didn't want to answer. I put my head on the glass and stared into the rain.

"Because when she wasn't talking to me, when she wasn't there, I talked to her friends too. When they called me worse things than an ogre and told me how much better off she was with this fairy tale prince of hers, I asked the only question that mattered."

"And they told you she was happy." Penny cocked her head. "That is it, isn't it? You... You would rather she was happy, than she was with you."

"Well, yeah. What else would I want for her?" I asked.

"So you didn't ring, or write, or try to set things right until she was in a weird place. Because the last thing she needed when she was madly, stupidly, gloriously in love with some young guy who makes her feel like a girl instead of a woman is... Well... The heartbroken ex."

"And when the friends back home ring her up, then yeah, they are going to think she needs to hear that I am a jerk, and I am an ass, and all that jazz, because otherwise she might stop and want to talk to me, and throw away her guy, who is not, all things considered, the bumbling moron I really, really, really wanted to believe him to be." I toasted her with a soda bottle. "Hence me, having the courage for just four dates, with three people, in the year I have been officially available. Not because I enjoy being alone and being miserable, but because... well, it turns out that changing the paint in a house doesn't make it my home instead of our home all that quickly."

"Has she seen it that way?" Penny asked. "I mean, has she ever thought to say sorry you may have been dead a week and I didn't notice until after the anniversary? Or is she still living a fairy tale?"

I shrugged. "She told her friends and the boyfriend I deserved better than our final confrontation in the street. A lot better than the week before the divorce. A hell of a lot better than a party to celebrate the divorce. Not like a mourning period or anything, but, why would you celebrate that? It wasn't like we were enemies rid of each other. It was just moving on. A toast maybe, but a party?"

"Maybe she deserves better than her friends in London." Penny whispered. "So, the wanting to be friends thing. Is that because you are worried how much baggage you carry, or that you aren't ready, or that the idea of being more than a friend with you is scary?"

I shook my head. "I wish I could tell you."

Penny sighed. "Don't say it like you are sorry. You were honest from when you made the offer. You were honest now. I asked the damned questions." She shook her head. "And I would rather hear you be honest than go home."

I smiled. "You don't have to tell me."

"No?"

"No." I looked out at the rain. "If you can't go home and I can help, then I can help."

She smiled. "Even if I ask stuff like this?"

"Is it really better than going home?" I asked.

She nodded.

"Then even if you ask that." I sipped my drink.

"You going to eat that?" She asked, pointing at my bag. I handed it to her and she unwrapped the second burger. She looked out into the rain as she ate. She chomped a mouthful from the bun and chewed on it thoughtfully. For a long while she didn't speak.

"So why here?" I asked.

She looked up from her burger.

"We could have had the burgers to eat in. Or I could have driven us to Reculver. The car park by the sea. With the old towers. I mean, I know it's just somewhere to eat. But..." I trailed off. She was smiling at me. "Because if I said something too stupid you could run for the bus stop here?"

She laughed. "No. Because there is no mobile phone signal here."

"Really?" I asked.

"You can check your phone." She finished the chicken burger. "Go on."

"I mean, that is really the reason? Why?" I swallowed. "So I can't call for help?"

"No." She smiled and put her hand back on my leg. It gave me a friendly pat. "And so we aren't disturbed when you get steamy. I just..." She caught herself before she said something. "I just wanted to talk to you and not be rung. You were being nice, and open, and I thought I could ask you anything, which I clearly can..." She smiled. "And if this is all we get from the evening, talking, you are cool with that. Which is a very good thing." She put the mischief back in her smile. "Not every night can be wild and carefree."

"For me this is wild and carefree." I said. "A woman I don't really know, somewhere lonely after a date, with nothing, but the rain..."

She smiled. "Want to know something?"

"Sure."

"I kind of wish I asked you to choose somewhere to go. The sea must be pretty spectacular in a storm like this." She looked out at the rain. "Waves smashing right up to the sea wall."

"Looks like a bad night to go fishing." I said. I remembered something from her profile. "Want to hear a ghost story?"

"Do you believe in ghosts?" She asked. Not saying yes or no, but trying to work out if I was taking this in a direction she was comfortable with.

I smiled at the question. "Not exactly. Maybe in a way. I believe there are all kinds of strange and wonderful experiences and somehow we lumped some together as something we call ghosts. I'm a sceptic, even after... Well... Kind of meeting one. "

"Okay." She looked at me. "Only kind of?"

"Stuff happens that people can't always explain right away. Sometimes it is psychological. Sometimes it is tricks of sound, or light, or imagination. Sometimes people lie, but when people experience stuff our brain looks for a way to explain it, and sometimes we come up with Ghost as the answer. Maybe we won't ever explain it, but that's it. We can't explain it." I said.

She smiled. "Ever find it weird that if you say something is unknown people always think they know what it is? Why a ghost. Why not an alien? Or an angel? Or a whole cloud of fairies?"

"I don't think any answer is more beautiful than saying I don't know. A mystery. I don't know what happened to me. If I was tricked, if it was all in my head. That is what makes it so cool." I said. I let it hang for a while. "Want to hear my story?"

"Yes." Penny nodded at me, enthusiastically.

"You know where the old cinema was in town?" I asked.

"Yeah." She laughed at the memory. "The old building near the market? I used to go in there all the time as a kid. The guys in the little blue waistcoats and bow ties right? So old fashioned but cute. And the smell of popcorn everywhere." She clicked her fingers. "And bees wax. There was all this ornate antique woodwork that always smelt of beeswax."

"I used to work there. As an usher, in a blue waistcoat. Bow tie."

"What?" She laughed. "No. I used to get in so much trouble there. The guys I hung around with when I was, what fourteen? Fifteen? They were the kind of guys who were a very long way from being criminal, but wanted to look dangerous and tough. So they figured the kids who worked there wanted their job too much to risk doing anything back if you threw popcorn, or swore, or goaded them. It's easy to look intimidating when you are asking somebody if they know who you are, and beating your chest, and telling them what a mug they are, if all they can do is throw you out."

I smiled. "I know."

"Oh crap." She laughed. It was sweet, and funny, but also embarrassed. "I once threw a litre of cola at one of those poor kids. Called him a..." She stopped laughing. "I don't want to tell you what I called him. You know the kid with the ginger hair and the acne?"

I nodded.

"Well I called him something and ran off. Giggling so much because I thought I was so daring, and the boys were so impressed and..." She stopped. "And when we were in the street later I was still giggly and funny, so one of the boys is mocking me, all sarcastic. I call him the same thing. He stares at me. What? So I laugh. A few others are laughing, but not so hard. Kind of nervous. I tell him that if he wants to be like that to me he's... One of the things I said." She shook her head. "It apparently wasn't so funny when it was said to him. He grabbed my throat. Told me that he didn't care if I had tits, a girl who speaks to him like that is a bitch and better be used to being hit. It... It made it all seem a lot less funny after that. Like... If it hurts them so bad they want to hit somebody why say it to another? Like how they would shove younger kids around for being goofy looking, but if anybody looked at their kid brother wrong there would be a fight. How can you know how bad something hurts and not think twice about hurting others? For what? Cleaning up our mess? Having a job? Not wanting to be useless?"

She put up her hands. "Sorry. I made myself the enemy, and I derailed a story."

"I was seventeen. Of course I had acne. And my hair was already darkening up, going more brown than red." I shook my head.

"I am so sorry." Penny wanted the seat to swallow her up.

"So one night I am doing the rounds after a show. Making sure the doors are all secured. There are no guests hanging around to be locked in. I went to knock on the doors of the bathrooms and as I approach the Ladies I can hear something behind the outermost door. So I knock. The door moves slightly against the frame. Something is pushing it closed from within, and I am sure I can hear giggling. So I announce we are closing, and ask if there is somebody there. I hear laughing, and it was absolutely clearly a laugh, the kind of kids like you playing hide and seek. But obviously I was meant to ask them to leave. Then the inner door is banging, too many times to be somebody just walking through. I think it is trouble makers, goading me, which is no big deal. So I walk in. I walk up to the inner door. And this time I hear a giggle again and see a shadow under the door. I hear the door pressing closed. I ask if they can just tell me they understood. The door releases, so I poke my head in, and I can see one of the stall doors closing. I can see a dark skirt under it. I can hear laughter. You know. Somebody playing around. Not somebody embarrassed at being caught short. So, I go up to the stall. I am about to knock on the door when it swings open."

"And?" Penny is trying not to look so awkward.

"Empty." I said.

She whistled.

"I see this empty stall. And I hear a giggle right behind me." I said. "So close I could feel her breath on the back of my neck. In the corner of my eye I am looking at the mirror and in the reflection I can see a shape. A shadow. Right behind my reflection. But when I turn, there is nothing. Nothing at all. I am alone."

"Scary." Penny said.

"No." I said, quietly. "It wasn't scary. I mean it wasn't a ghost trying to make me jump out of my skin. It was girl, trying to be... I don't know. Playful. Or cute. Just a kid." I felt uneasy. "It wasn't scary because it was gone. It was scary because if there was some kind of ghost, then it meant there was some poor little girl who was... Well... You know."

Penny nodded. She looked distant for a moment. She shuffled away from me, cramming herself against the door and reaching around to open it. She paused as she watched the storm, and seemed frozen, unable to decide on if she was fleeing or not. She squinted at the clock on the supermarket, the glowing green display.

"Your clock is three minutes fast." She said, weakly. "Like, you don't ever want to be late. Or always want to be a little early." She gave a snort of a laugh and shook her head.

"You okay?" I asked.

"Yeah." She turned the smile full of mischief back on. But her eyes were a little distant, they were sparkling in the dim light of the car park. She checked her phone again.

"How often do you have to do this?" I asked. "To be here so you can't get called."

She gave me a vague gesture as an answer. "Oh you know..."

"Because, if you want, I could bring coffee from the all night place, a latte each, one of those oversized custard biscuits they do..." I trailed off as I ran out of confidence. "If you just wanted some company who.. you know... didn't think the lonely corner was somewhere to come to play around."

She gave me an expression I could not read and leaned over. She put a hand to my chest, and kept leaning. I could feel her breath on me, on my lips, a few moments before her eyes closed and it became a kiss. All those nerve endings in my lips electrifying under the gentlest of caresses. My heart thundered so hard I thought it was going to shatter.

She drew her lips back. She smiled and her blush deepened as she saw my dazed expression.

"That did not feel like a no." I said.

"You are sweet." Penny whispered. "You don't see it in yourself. The way you tell your story and try so hard not to blame your ex, and say nobody was really at fault. You don't believe that. Deep down you think you were a monster, who only really made her happy by leaving her alone. And you are wrong. I mean maybe you are right, that she is happy now, and right that nobody should be blamed when people just fall out of love. But wrong about being a monster. You are sweet." She stopped herself. "I want to say yes. I really want to. I thought you were going to be..." She closed her eyes. She looked for a second like somebody had punched her in the stomach. "You really would just come and sit in my car with me while I stared at the clock and counted the minutes?"

"Would it be better than being alone?" I asked.

She nodded.

"Then yes. I would. But if not, can I see you again after tonight anyway?"

She screwed her face up into a frown. She swore under her breath. "Can you drive me home? I live on the Briar Green Estate. Marlow Road."

I started the engine. The radio turned on as I did. Radio Four had given way to the world service for the late hours. We drove out into the rain and through the estate. It was a dense knot of houses built in the seventies. Brick terraces, some still looking brand new, most a little weathered, and some looking a lot worse for wear. The estate had a bad reputation, a notoriety, that was only deserved by one or two of the households. A notoriety that was fading as the company who owned many of the houses redeveloped them and rented them to new tenants.

"This is me." She said, nodding at one of the houses. I pulled over and parked. She closed her eyes for a few moments. "I'm sorry." She looked around her. "For this. I am. It..."

"It's fine." I said gently. "If it is something you need to do... You know my number."

She nodded.

"You don't have to see me again." I said. "I wasn't much fun either. If you want to call me, or text me, or whatever. If not... I understand."

She smiled at me. It was not a smile with any mischief or humour. She leaned over and she kissed me again. It was a little less of a shock. It was warm, and gentle, and there was a giddy novelty in the idea of somebody wanting to kiss me that almost made my teeth chatter.

"In case this is goodbye." Penny said, as she withdrew. "I have... I have so much I need to think about. I'm sorry. I don't know."

She plunged out of the car and into the rain, before I knew what to say.

TWO

Saturday morning woke me, when the low winter sun found the crack between my curtains and cast a slither of sharp light across my bed. I rolled over to shield my eyes and reached out to the far side of the bed. The mattress was cold and empty, a shock to the system that knocked me awake and back to reality. I blinked. Pickles, my stuffed badger now lived on the pillow on the other side of the bed. I felt weird talking to the shadows when I couldn't sleep and needed to empty the fuzz and the noise of the thoughts from my head. I felt a little less weird talking to something that had eyes and a face, even if it was made from patchwork and came from the craft market.

"So did that date go as terrible as I think?" I asked.

Pickles gave me a blank stare.

"You think if she calls me, it means it didn't go so bad?"

Pickles had nothing to say on the matter.

"Okay. If it went well, I need to celebrate with good coffee. If it went terrible, then good coffee eases the pain." I grinned at the denim and velveteen badger. "I am making coffee." I rolled back to my side of the bed and sat up. Pain exploded in my side. A white hot lance of pain that reached through my flesh and scraped on my ribs. It hit me so hard and fast it knocked the air from my lungs and made me dizzy.

I howled out and looked down at my side. Blood caked my side and stained my sheets. The sight of it made me dizzy, fireworks detonating behind my eyes. I took a moment for the shock to finish echoing through my bones, then I walked quickly to the bathroom. I found a flannel and washed the blood away. Each touch of the cloth left me in agony, making the pain flash and my jaw set. There was a circular graze surrounded by a mottled pattern of black, blue, purple and green. The dark core of the bruise was the size of my palm. The green tinge spread further. Out as far as I could spread my fingers.

I touched the bruise. The pain made my stomach want to empty into my throat. I swallowed it back and had to lean on the sink to stay up the right way. I closed my eyes and waited for the pain to stop echoing through my bones. My jaw set. Panic and pain was making my heart pound. I could feel my lungs heaving to draw breath. I breathed too deep, the pain was fresh and sharp. I fell back onto the towel rail.

I slumped to the floor and sat there a good long while. I steadied my breath and tried to think. I tried to think how the bruise got there, and my thoughts kept coming up empty. It was easier to think on what I needed to do. I got to my knees, then my feet, found my phone and went down to the kitchen. I flicked the address book on my phone and scrolled down to Lex. My phone is clogged with numbers. A legion of contacts, a few actual friends. Lex was always the best of them.

"Birdie?" Lex sounded confused and sleepy.

"I am so sorry to wake you." I said. "To call even. I..."

"No." She filled the word with honey and sherbet. "No you have to call. You have to tell me about the date."

"Lex. I don't know what happened. My side is all bruised, I think I cracked a rib, and there was blood." I tried to sound calm. "It hurts and I can't drive myself to A&E. I need a lift."

"Oh." She laughed. "Does that mean the date went real well, or real bad?"

"It hurts to breathe." I said. "I'm not asking you as a doctor. Just a mate."

She laughed again, but this time it was nervous. "It hurts?"

"I can't drive myself to hospital. If you can't make it then I will get a taxi." I said.

"Do you have any of the good coffee in?" She no longer sounded sleepy.

*

Half an hour later the coffee was brewed and Lex was in my kitchen, gesturing for me to lift up my tee shirt. She was a kind woman with skin like polished teak and maple brown eyes. Her hair would have been wild if it wasn't tied back and tamed by a number of decorative clips. Her smile was always bright and youthful. Even when it was thin and trying to hide the worry on her face.

"Date went real bad then?" She whispered.

"The date went okay. I don't know how this happened." I said.

"You didn't notice the guy with the tyre iron beating on you?" She looked stunned. "Birdie, please. Mate to mate, Doctor to patient, tell me what happened and it stays here. Did the nice girl from the dating site do something?"

"We met for coffee. We watched the film. We went to a car park and ate a take away because she didn't want to go home." I said. "Only painful thing there was when she asked about the divorce and I didn't know how to stop talking."

She put some plastic gloves on and prodded the bruise. She rummaged in her bag for an adhesive dressing. I clenched my jaw to stop me howling. Lex winced and tutted. "Whatever did this, you must have noticed? Did things get kinky? In the heat of the moment, you may not have noticed how hard her knee was digging in. Or a few knocks? No? Okay. Did somebody roll you over for a wallet? Birdie, if somebody kicked you in, I won't think any less of you. You never were a fighter."

"No."

"Okay." She frowned at me. "Did you fall down the stairs? Throw yourself out of bed somehow?"

I shook my head.

"If it was anybody else I would ask how much you drank." She said. She closed her eyes and paused for a moment. "Are you still taking pills to help you sleep?"

"Not for months." I said.

"Then if you fell out of bed this would have woken you." She put a hand on my shoulder. She looked at me, direct into my eyes. "Okay. Whatever you aren't telling me, the bruise will fade, but it is going to take some time. Do you have pain killers?"

I nodded. "I don't like to-"

"I know." She let me pour her a coffee, and helped herself to one of the cakes I had left in the basket on the kitchen counter. "You really don't know?"

"No." I said.

"Is..." She sipped her coffee and tried not to look too worried. "Is everything okay? I mean, have you been feeling down? Stressed?" She paused. "Is there anything I need to know? As a friend. As a doctor." She sipped her coffee. "As somebody who saw you at your worst."

I shook my head. "Apart from the mystery bruise, I am fine. I feel stupid for calling you now."

She was rummaging in the kitchen drawer and held up the packet of pain killers she found. She frowned, trying to decide if they were strong enough. "Stupid, why? You had to be sure."

"I think the blood scared me." I said.

She put her coffee down and looked at the bedding in the washing machine. "It doesn't take much blood to make a big mess. Believe me." She smiled. "You really are shaken up aren't you?"

"Well, imagine waking up with this and not knowing how it got there." I said.

"I can't." She chomped down on her cake. "You can work from home for a few days?"

I nodded.

"You okay, if I keep an eye on you now and again?" She asked.

"Sure." I smiled. "I- Thank you Lex. You are a godsend. Sorry. How are things with you?"

She laughed. "I'm fine. I was up in the Smoke for the last few days. I saw Jean and Troy. Had a good meal out. It was nice."

"How is she?"

"Good." Lex carefully measured her smile. "She is good. Really excited for Christmas, and her job is well and truly flying."

"Brilliant." I eased into a chair and drank my coffee. I didn't look at Jean's social media. She had blocked me before the divorce. Back when she was just ignoring me. When we did talk, she asked me to block her too. Lex was still friends with both of us, and had never felt the need to pick sides. I let myself be hopeful. "So she is happy?"

"Happy?" Lex thought on it a while. "I think so. Sometimes it is a bit difficult for her, and then I think she misses what you used to have. Troy is great, a real good guy, but remember what we were like at his age? He is still making all the mistakes we already learned from, and he thinks he is already grown up so he doesn't know they are mistakes. Jean has all the patience in the world for him, but it isn't always easy."

"Is there anything I could do?" I coughed. "They don't need to know it was me."

"No." Lex took a top up. She said it with a smile. "They are doing good. I promise. Hand over heart, she is fine." Her hand did not go anywhere near her heart.

I nodded. For a few seconds we both believed it.

"Just one thing she said got to me." She said at last.

"Do I want to know?"

"She's excited for Christmas. She is spending it up in the Highlands with Troy's family." Lex said. "Which is great. I love how quickly she got so close to them. But she told me it was the first time she ever had a family to love, or to love her. Because you know what her own family were like."

I smiled. "I'm glad. She deserves to feel like that."

"I know. But it made so little of your family. Of stuff I lived through right beside her. She didn't mean to offend. I don't think she saw that it got to me. But..." She smiled and dropped another couple of the muffins in a napkin for her pocket. "But she is happy."

"Good." I nodded. "But I mean it. If she needs help..."

"Oh." Lex thought on her words. "Birdie, please, I love that you would always offer to help. But don't. Not for Jean. I love her to bits, I really do, but she can't see you. Not like this."

"I'm not about to steal her back." I said.

"No." Lex paused, her voice dropping. "Birdie, look, she knows she did as many things to hurt you as she always said you did to her. It already eats her up. But she had Troy to fall in love with and that did more to keep her together than she would ever believe. She never saw how far you fell. She never saw the state you got yourself in when you had nobody. If she sees you now, if she sees all the weight you lost, the beard. If she just looks in your eyes. She will know. Anybody else might believe you just had a diet and walked more often, but she would know. She would see this is where you climbed back up to, she will work out how far she made you fall." She ran a finger over my cheek. "This would break her. She could stand the guilt of murder more than she could stand the guilt of this. Don't offer to help."

I nodded. "I guess she won't ask anyway."

Lex smiled. She shook her head and cast away the serious nature of the last few minutes. "So, tell me about the date. Tell me how badly she fell for you and how desperate she will be to see you again?" She nursed her coffee and listened intently as I told her as much as I knew about Penny, and pretty much everything we had talked about.

"She kissed you twice?" Lex grinned. "See. Not getting a kiss is not always a bad sign. Getting a kiss is a good sign. That she liked the kiss and wanted an encore is brilliant. It means she was thinking if she could invite you in, or if she should leave you wanting more. You only do that when you want more yourself. Maybe not right away, but still on the table."

"You think?" I asked.

"I think." Lex grinned. "I think she was a little upset that you went somewhere to talk and not go home and all you did was talk. Like she had a baby sitter or something and wanted fun where she could get it."

"It wasn't like that." I said.

"No." Lex shook her head. "Doesn't mean the thought didn't occur to her."

"It really wasn't like that." I said.

"Then it's even better." Lex patted my back. "It means she wants more than just...wanting more. She wants something that it is worth taking her time to find."

I finished my coffee and started to clear up, dissembling the coffee machine into the dishwasher and stacking the cups. Lex crossed the kitchen and leaned herself on the counter, close to me. She put a hand on my wrist.

"Birdie. I'm glad you tried this. Okay. Even if you only signed up for me. I'm glad." She kissed my cheek. "I really do want this to work out for you."

I was supposed to find something to say. I couldn't. All the words got jammed in my head. So I nodded and looked down at her long fingers on my wrist. "Thanks for stopping by. I... I didn't know what else to do. Who else to ask."

"It's no trouble. Just take it easy today. Let me know if isn't getting better in a few days once the graze scabs over."

I nodded.

"Good. See. The Birdie who smiles is the Birdie I like." She kissed my cheek. "Tell you what. If you feel bad about it, I'm having some friends for tea and coffee on Tuesday, lunch time to mid-afternoon. Promise me one of those cakes with the apples in the middle, or a tea loaf, and I will consider myself paid. It's for a charity fighting cancer. Kind of sponsored."

"Of course. Anything." I made a mental note to add some ingredients to pick up.

"Great. Then can I owe you a favour too?" She made big eyes at me. "I was going to get my cards out. But if you felt like showing off..."

I nodded. "I can do that too."

Lex beamed, her smile on full power.

*

I took it easy for the day. I got comfortable on the sofa and marked a whole bunch of essays. Year eights views on an obscure corner of the crusades. Most wrote with considerably less enthusiasm than they showed the Knights Templar at the start of the term. I hammered out a few reports, and got my virtual paperwork well ahead of schedule. I paced around the kitchen and I tried not to think about when or if my phone would call. I tried to find ways to keep me still, to stop me rushing to the shops for heavy bags of flour and sugar, or taking a walk. Everything I felt I should have done would have meant feeling the pain in my side.

At ten in the evening I felt like I was dragging chains and caskets, weighed down by exhaustion. The late night, and the panic of the morning had both taken their toll. I flicked the TV off and set the burglar alarm early. I took a couple of pain killers before I climbed the wooden hill to Bedfordshire, nursing my side with every step and tumbled onto the first cloud to the land of nod.

As soon as I lay my head to the pillow I felt like I was falling into dark waters and descending to the depths, as a dreamless, haunted, sleep claimed me.

*

On Sunday the strange mark on my side was feeling a little better. A little less raw and fresh. It was a constant dull pain rather than a cacophony of stabbing pains. Some of the purple and blue was turning to the green and yellow as the edges retreated. But the graze was tacky and sickly. The edges were red, and there was a glassy, caramel scab covering it. It hurt to breathe, but it was a duller, bass note of a pain. So I dressed and I made myself go to the shops, before I felt too much of a prisoner in my own home. I figured I would have to use a trolley, and pack the groceries in many bags that I could ferry along the drive in a few trips, to save too much strain on my side.

I parked at the supermarket and stared across the car park to the furthest corner. I checked my phone again and saw no messages, no emails, and no calls. No signal. I dragged myself from the car and armed myself with a trolley. I took my time, stocking up on apples, dried fruit, sugar, flour, honey, some spices, and some other stuff I use a lot of in the kitchen, some milk, cheese, and everything I needed to make my favourite pasta sauce. I aimed for the pharmacy aisle last, to grab some dressings and pain killers.

"Oh my God." The words were so close behind me they almost made me jump. I looked around. Penny was there with a hand basket. It was a light load. A newspaper and three chocolate bars. She was frowning at the pile of dressings. "Are you going to war?"

"Fancy dress as the Mummy?" I offered. She gave me a pity laugh for the joke. "I managed to fall over at home and must have caught myself on the bed."

"Ouch." Penny widened her eyes. "You going to be okay with all that?"

"I can manage, I think." I felt my throat dry up. "It's good to see you again. I mean, good you spoke to me and didn't run off to hide. Or escape."

"Yeah. Well. I just stalked you from the dairy section. I kept arguing with myself if I should say hi, or hint you should ask me out, or just ask when to see you, or run away." Penny let the words out in a rapid babble. They bounced off each other in the hurry to get out. "And if I waited to get home I would be a coward. Especially as I followed you rather than rush for the bus, you know?"

"So, do you have plans for lunch?" I asked.

"Yeah." She nodded at the chocolate. "But they are very, very, bad plans. I am always open to being bought lunch."

I looked at the stuff I had for the pasta. More than I would need, even if I had left overs in the evening. I gave her a smile. "Oh. Bought lunch? I meant if I was going to cook?"

Penny started to nod her head with enthusiasm. "Yeah. I would like that. At yours?"

"Yeah." I said. "If that would be okay?"

She kept nodding. I took her basket and lay it in the trolley. She followed me to the tills, and spoke about the movie we saw. Her eyes brightened with enthusiasm as she found her comfort zone talking about the film, which lead to comic books, which lead to myths and legends.

When we got back to mine she helped me carry the shopping in and wandered around the kitchen and dining room, a dreamy smile on her face, sipping sparkling water from a glass full of ice chips as I cooked. She looked at the two watercolours by the stairs.

"Are those the ones that caused so much trouble?" She asked.

"No." I shook my head. "Those ones are up in the bedroom." I pointed my knife at the matching pair on the stairs. They were small, each only the size of a post card. Both were of the same oak tree. One in autumn, the other in spring. "Those I bought a few months back to liven up the place a little." I thought it best not to mention there used to be photos on that wall I didn't want to look at any more. She walked around and looked at the other large frame that decorated a blank wall. It was a framed set of tarot cards, each with a unique image on. Hand drawn. The images were crude, messy, copies of designs that had been beautiful when rendered by more talented hands.

"Oh." She reached up and almost touched the glass, drawing her fingers back.

"The first set I drew myself." I said. "You can buy packs from a shop, but to do things right I was always taught to use my own. It makes it more personal. I bought blanks, so the patterns on the back are identical, and spent ages drawing them."

She looked over her shoulder at me. "I thought you were a sceptic? About ghosts and stuff."

"Yes." I said with a smile. "I like history. I like folk lore and traditions. I like ghost stories and I like mysteries."

"I know what you mean." Penny stared, fascinated by the cards. "I like conspiracy theories. I don't know why I always read books about them, because I never believe them. But yet I adore them."

"Tarot has a lot of history. Seventy eight cards, originally from the fifteenth century, originally used for games. They became a mystic device in the eighteenth century. The mystical side has a lot of traditions. I like those." I smiled. "I have some other decks I prefer to use for readings, if you wanted me to show you that some time."

"Okay." She said with a smile. "To tell me you can't tell me anything?"

"Oh. I think they can tell us stuff. But by purely Earthly means I am afraid. They offer us a random pattern, and the human mind is evolved to see patterns in the random, and a meaning in the pattern."

"There are a lot more cards than I thought." She said.

"That kind was used for playing games. Just like playing cards today. The kind you see in films are decks produced by more modern magicians, just for predictions." I left the sauce to simmer as I started to carve bread from a loaf. "I can show you a magician's deck later. The same kind you would buy in a shop, but again, drawn by own hand. Like tradition."

She nodded and helped me set out some places at the table. She looked at the carved head of the green man I decorated my kitchen cupboard with. An antique salvaged from a manor house.

"He used to live in a church?" She asked.

"No. But many like him did. The green man." I explained.

"Like with Morris Dancers?" She smiled and walked over to it. As I spooned pasta and sauce into the bowls she ran her fingers over the carving, examining every facet, every leaf and vine.

"Yes." I said with a smile. "The personification of the wild forest. Fallow nature."

"More tradition." She said.

I nodded.

"So why the cards?" She said. We sat and we ate.

"It's in my family. Fortune tellers, psychics, mediums. Mum and Nan would always tell me these stories that go with the cards. Explanations of how they could tell the future, of what the cards meant, and of what the cards could tell you. But I could never get to grips with astrology or palmistry. But I could work with cards. I could work with maths, with sleights of hand. My job is dull as dishwater. I work in a school. I teach. History. I read reports. I grade papers. I worry about details nobody wants to hear or can stand to hear for five minutes. When I come home from work, even if I am only coming up from the office in the cellar, I like to have something colourful, something lively to do. I could keep bees, or learn to paint. But I can make cakes and buns that are good enough for mates if not to sell."

"And pasta which is yummy." Penny said.

"Thanks. And I did stuff with the cards. I make decks. I do readings. I do tricks. I learned some related stuff. I'm no expert. I just like the subject." I smiled. "I like to look under the hood and see how all the little bits work."

"I collect ghost stories." She said. Her eyes fixed on mine. "Real ghost stories that people tell. I e-mail people who have stories. I ask if they can tell it in their own words for the site. Like an oral history, but with e-mails. Not just e-mails. Weird stories in general."

"Do you believe them?" I asked.

"You mean do I believe yours?" She smiled. "What was it you said about the most beautiful answer being to admit you don't know?"

I smiled.

"It's my escape. I come home from work and I need to not think about work. I need to do something else so my brain can get distracted and potter away at work in the background, so I can sleep at night and not dream of work. So I collect ghost stories. I wish I could cook too." She held up a fork with some pasta on the end. "I love this."

We fell into silence for a while. I hadn't eaten like that, having somebody just enjoy the food, to enjoy my company without a reason, for too long. She glanced up and smiled.

"So what happens with the reading?" She asked.

"It depends what cards I use. But I will ask you to shuffle the cards. To breathe on them. Then I will deal some. If I use my favourite cards I will deal three pairs. Each pair will describe something about you. Something that is happening right now. And we will see how well the cards know you." I shrugged. "If you want."

"Yeah." She smiled. "I want to. Do I get to see you draw cards too?"

"You think it will tell you something about me?" I asked. "Okay."

She seemed happy with that. When she finished her bowl, a second bowl, and bread, I put the left overs in the fridge, the pans in the dishwasher and showed her through to the living room.

She stared at the two framed playing cards. A king of hearts and a queen of hearts, side by side.

"Something from the marriage?" She asked.

I shook my head. For a second I almost told her more. But she was looking at the cards with a thin smile. She cocked her head and stroked her chin.

"No. I put that up after." I smiled. "There is a game in the picture. I'll show you some other time. But it you want to do the reading, now would be good. I need a little practise."

She looked back to me and smiled.

The smile stole the words from my lips, and the beat of my heart.

THREE.

I dug through some decks in the drawer. I smiled and found my Masterpiece Deck. The cards were in two bundles. The Minor Arcana were fifty six cards, a lot like playing cards. There were swords, wands, coins and cups, numbered one to ten, then Page, Knight, Queen and King. I set those to one side and started to shuffle the Major Arcana, the picture cards that most people imagine as a tarot deck. Twenty two cards. Twenty one are numbered, the Fool is not. I don't know if Penny noticed, or was impressed that I shuffled the cards so when I fanned them out for her to look at, they were in number order. Juggler (I am old fashioned, I have a Juggler not a Magician), Priestess, Empress, Emperor, Hierophant, Lovers, Chariot, Strength, Hermit, Wheel, Justice, Hanged Man, Death, Temperance, Devil, Tower, Star, Moon, Sun, Judgement, and the World.

"You drew these?" She asked.

I nodded. "As close as I could to the way they are always drawn. In the fifteenth century, all had to be hand drawn. It was part of learning the trade." I watched as she picked up the Lovers. "There are a few different patterns, and artists make new images for decks all the time. But for this deck tradition is the key. I drew it in my own hand, but had to have all the key elements there. Like how if you look at normal playing cards, you know the King, Queen and Jack because they almost always look a certain way. Like a code. So that card has to have Adam and Eve, a fruit tree, an angel looking over them, offering a choice. It does not have to mean love, or sex, if upright, it can mean a choice that when made will be irreversible. Turn it the other way and it is a choice you can not back down on." I showed her the Devil. I lifted it out and put it down for her to look at as she held the Lovers. "See how the same pair appear with the devil. But here they carry all the suits of tarot, the grapes are coins, the fire is the wand, his wings are air, which represents the swords. All he misses is the chalice or cup. He is missing the sign of kindly blessing."

Penny nodded. She looked at the World. A naked woman dancing in the clouds, with a ring of leafs around her, and the heads of a human, an eagle, a lion and an ox watching her. Penny gave me a smile that asked the question. So I pointed to each of the heads in turn.

"If you are Christian these are Matthew, Mark, Luke, and John. Or perhaps Aquarius, Scorpio, Leo and Taurus. But if you are a real Christian Scholar you will call these animals surrounding something the Throne of Ezekiel. But it means contentment, blessing, and eternal joy. Endless hope."

I paused.

"What?" Penny asked.

"The two cards you hold. It is a very powerful combination. It came up once, when we were at a fair and Jean, knowing me too well, insisted we got a reading from the nice lady in a booth. She drew a seven card hand for Jean. Looking over it was the Star. Hope, Optimism, Trust." I put the Star in place. Seven little stars surrounding a blazing gold eight pointed star, in whose light Eve filled chalices from the river and poured a chalice onto the land. She had one foot in the water, one on the land.

"You said water was a blessing, for the cups?" She asked.

"The water is the Universal, or God, the Spirit. It is a creative blessing. The land is the material world. Practical and pragmatic. So both sides of nature are under a bright light, and both are being blessed by her chalices. Like the holy grail?" I said.

She nodded. "Hope. Optimism. Trust. And a big old bird."

"Ibis."

"Cool." She grinned.

"On the left hand were the Goddess, who indicates a prosperity, maternal kindness, comfort and power." I put the card in place. "And the Priestess. Who is wisdom, common sense, love and intuition. On the right hand was the Sun," I set down the card that showed a babe on a horse with the sun above him. "Who is innocence, radiance, growth, and happiness. And the tower upside down. Which mean crisis, and discomfort, downfall and dissolution, but upside down means in the past. It is overcome."

"Kindness overcame despair." Penny said.

I nodded. "And across her heart were those two cards." I pointed at her hands.

"Lovers, so this really can mean love? Sex? Relationships?" Penny said. "And with this, eternal hope and joy, that has to mean true love?"

"It doesn't have to." I said. "But that is one meaning. The more literal meaning is that she will always be loved. When we walked away from the reading she knew I saw something a little different."

Penny smiled and put the cards back.

"So I told her." I said, quietly. "She asked what the difference was, but I said it didn't matter."

"This is the kind of reading I want." Penny said.

"Okay." I nodded and swept the cards up. I started to shuffle. I handed her the deck. "Could you shuffle these? So I am not tempted to pull any tricks."

She took the cards, gave me a look of mock suspicion, shuffling the cards, cutting and splicing the deck. She went to hand them back.

"No. Blow on the deck first." I said.

"Blow?" She frowned.

"Well I don't think I know you well enough to ask you to kiss the deck." I said.

She lifted the cards to her lips. Blew on the cards gently and teasingly. Then kissed it. She set it on the table and I lifted the first seven from the deck. A head. A pair on the left hand, the right hand, and the pair on the heart. I set them face down.

I turned over the head card first.

"The devil." Penny gave me a weak smile.

"The devil can represent temptation, desire, or a passion." I tapped the card with a finger. "Here on the head it means you have something to which you are bound. A goal or an ambition that restrains you. Sometimes a vice, but often something perfectly good, perfectly normal, that you have allowed to dominate you."

She closed her eyes. She looked sad. "I am pretty sure that is true."

I smiled. "What would you like to know next? The heart, is pretty much what you expect, what you hold in your heart, your spirit. The left hand is your subconscious. It is where the spirit world or the dreams can connect to you. The right is your strength. Your virtue. How you impact upon the world. Left hand tells us how the world is shaping us, the right hand is how we shape our world."

"Left hand first." She whispered.

I turned the cards over.

"The hanged man." I said. "It can mean conformity. Or Acceptance. But on the left hand it is often a sign of sacrifice." I turned over the next card. "The tower. Crisis. Hubris. But above all change. This pair together can mean mourning, or it can mean the acceptance of a change, a disruption, that can-not be undone. Words that can't be unsaid, an action that can't be undone. But you can move on and find peace."

She nodded.

"To be free of the devil." I said.

She smiled at that, for a moment it was a very sad smile. "I hope so."

"Right hand next?" I asked.

She nodded. I turned the cards over.

"The Fool. Upside down. Normally he means a free spirit. But upside down he means a risk taker. Reckless. Abandon." I pointed to the next. "And the King. Upside down. Order, tradition, authority, all upside down. The world holds you back, but you would do anything to be free."

She smiled. "Even internet dating."

"Ready to see what is in your heart?" I asked.

She smiled. "I'm ready to see what you think is in my heart."

I turned over the first card. "Strength." I said. "Fortitude, resolution, but also gentleness. Strength is not pride. It is not domination. It is something more subtle and positive."

She nodded.

I turned over the next card. "And the World. Eternal hope, joy. Your Strength will never be diminished. No matter what."

She covered her lips and she shook her head. "I wish that were true. I really do." She tapped the cards. "But the devil who sits on my shoulder has not made life easy." She tapped the left hand. "And he is not so easy to make my peace with."

"Do you want to talk about it?" I asked.

"No." She ran her finger along the cards. "It's not something I could talk about."

"Okay." I picked the cards up and shuffled them. "Just tell me how to help."

"Just like that." She said it with a childish smile. Then she softened her tone. "You'll just throw yourself in at the deep end, hide in a car park and not ask what we are hiding from? Or if I deserve the company?"

I concentrated on the cards. Once upon a time, when things were still fresh and new between me and Jean she fell off her bike. She didn't hurt herself bad, but she was shaken up and bruised. She rang me barely able to breathe, promising me she was okay, and she was safe, and telling me not to worry or to rush to her, in a way I was stupid enough to believe that meant I should not panic, or rush to be with her.

I tried to get my work in order. I set everything in order around the office. I tried to get in a place I could go to be with her, rather than just dropping everything and running to her immediately. It was an hour later that Lex rang me and informed me that I was a colossal arse.

Getting home. Seeing Jean pale as a sheet, caked in sweat, with ice packs on a swollen and bruised arm, still hearing the squeal of the brakes from the truck that almost swept her off the road. My heart stopped.

If there is a hell, it is an eternity of that split second when you realise you failed to be there for the person you loved when they were in pain you can-not imagine. It is absolute despair of failing them.

It is a hell I will not visit again.

"Just like that." I said.

"I showed you mine." Penny whispered, teasingly. She patted the table.

I shuffled the cards with no trick or plan. I let the cards fall where they may. I lay out my seven cards. My head, left hand, right hand and my heart between them. Silently I turned over the head. The Hermit. Solitude, isolation, and introspection.

"What do you think it means?" I asked.

"I don't know the cards." She laughed.

"Just look at the name, and the picture and tell me what you think it would mean. If you were telling a story. Anything that you think suits the picture."

"You are a bit of an exile." She put a hand to my cheek. "I think you have been stuck in your head for too long."

"I think that is fair enough." I turned over the left hand, to see what the world had in store for me. Death and the Devil danced together. One was change, the other a binding restraint, together they were an ill omen. "And this?"

Penny met my eyes. They were full of pathos and sorrow. "You worry too much about the past."

I reached over to the right hand. The juggler was upside down. He should have meant skill and cunning. Upside down he was a manipulator. He was paired with the Hanged Man.

"The Hanged Man was sacrifice." Penny said. She gave me a warm laugh. "Oh come on, I've known you ten minutes and I already know you will throw your cloak over a puddle for just about anybody. I think the cards are calling you gallant."

I turned over my heart cards. The Emperor and High Priestess upside down. He was warning of domination, of a rigid order imposed on me. She whispered of hidden agendas and conspiracy.

"I don't know what it means." Penny said.

"That my heart is not my own." I whispered.

"Oh." Penny giggled. "In a good way?"

"I hope so." I said. "It could be, I guess."

"But it suggests something else?" She asked.

"It's more that something can control the heart by force. Perhaps somebody will do something that means I am compelled a certain way, or that circumstances will tower over me so I am forced to act against my character. Life is like that. Sometimes there are no easy answers and our heart can not be our own." I said it gently, but Penny was looking pale. She drew her hand away from me and chewed on her lip. "I'm sorry. Have I...said something wrong?"

She shook her head. "No. It just made me think of something."

"It's what the cards are for." I smiled. She did not.

"I should go." She whispered. "I do not think I should have come at all."

"Penny." I put a hand on her knee. She clamped it there under a clammy palm, cold and frigid with fear. She gripped my hand so tight, that her knuckles bleached and her nails dug into my skin. "If I stumbled onto something that touched a nerve. I am sorry. I know you don't like to talk about things, and I have done nothing to earn your trust yet, but if..."

"Don't." She shook her head. "Sorry. But don't ask to help. Don't tell me you will be here for me. Don't..." She put her hand on my shoulder to hold me back, as she stood. "My life is so full of trouble. I thought doing this would let me forget a while. The guys I meet are nice, the dates are fun, but it never works out. They all find reasons to lose touch long before my troubles catch up with them. But you are the wrong kind of nice." She frowns. "I know that makes no kind of sense, but you can't do this. You can't worry for me. It will be..." She clenched a fist. "You were meant to be just another one of the married guys looking to play around in shallow waters. Somebody who would help if asked be grateful not to know too much. I wasn't even meant to like you too much."

"What kind of trouble?" I asked, but she was walking for the front door. Running. I got up and followed her. In my head I was imagining all kinds of trouble watching over her. Abusive ex boyfriends, with a jealous streak and a temper. She was out the front door just as the heavens cracked open and the afternoon filled with a thick slurry of rain. I slipped into some shoes and grabbed my waterproof jacket. I followed her out of the house. As I pulled the door closed behind me she was at the street, wrapping her arms around her and looking left and right, trying to choose a way to go, trying to plan the quickest path to her own front door.

"Penny." I said, as I approached, holding the jacket.

"Don't touch me." She snapped. I froze and looked at my hands, they were still holding the coat. "No." She softened her voice. "I didn't mean that." She smiled at the old lady on the other side of the pavement. "I didn't mean it like that love!" She looked back to me. "Don't touch me. Don't hold me. Don't tell me I'm going to be okay." She laughed, it was a strained, haunted sound. "I already want those too much."

"Take the coat." I said as softly as I could. "Before you catch a death."

She took the coat, hung it over her like a cloak.

"If you won't want a lift, will you let me ring for a taxi?" I asked. I looked away from her eyes. "I'm trying not to be nice. But this is getting me worried, right here, right now. If you don't want to see me, or hear from me, or anything again, whatever the reason, then please, let me get you a taxi. I know a company around the corner, and I am fairly sure the drivers aren't the unlicensed kind you read about in True Crime Nightmares. Okay?"

She smiled. "And you can change the locks and start shopping at the other supermarket?"

I handed her my phone. "Delete your number. Check it's gone. Block me on the dating site."

"And you will forget about me?" She said, trying to smile.

"I will spend far too long worrying I should have done something more." I admitted. "But I'll respect your wishes. If I haven't earned your trust, I won't bully you." I stepped back. "If you want to give me a chance to earn my trust you can give my coat back some time. I... I've been working from home a lot these last few months. You have my number, or I have a doorbell." I could see her about to complain again, so I put my hands up. "Only if you need me. If you need a friend, a phone you can call a shelter from, or call your solicitor from, or anything. Okay?"

"Bollocks." Penny stamped her foot and stepped forwards. She leant up and kissed me, her lips prying mine apart so our breath would mingle as she dropped my phone back to my hand. She put her arms around me and squeezed me in a hug. The old lady over the road looked like she approved, her scowl lost in the rain, right up until I let out a yelp of pain. Penny was hugging me on my wound. I felt like a lightning bolt had hit my spine, my knees buckling. For a moment I was dizzy.

"Bollocks!" Penny repeated, her voice climbing an octave.

"I'm okay. Just a bruise." I said, through gritted teeth.

Penny stared at me, her eyes bulging in horror, then ran off, my coat on her shoulders, the hood up. I tried to call out to her, but the pain meant all I could make was a dry rasp as I heaved for a breath. I watched her vanish around the corner at a sprint, and then I ducked back into the house.

FOUR

I sat on the edge of the bed, my head too full to sleep.
The echoes of my time with Penny still bouncing around my head
like rubber ball. I was haunted by the warmth of her smile. By
the way it was so easy to speak to her. So natural to laugh with
her. And by the worries I now held for her. I wondered how
much respect I would have for her wishes, when I was watching
a Police Re-enactment of her last movements and explaining
that no, I deleted her number and didn't push her for answers.

Because I was afraid I would push too hard and hurt her.

"I'm an idiot Pickles." I said.

The badger was in no rush to answer. I looked up at the
watercolours on the wall over my chest of drawers. Simple
drawings, a few strokes of a pen and some pale washes
suggesting terraces of shops in a market town. Tall, austere,
Victorian buildings, with large display windows and hand painted
signs, on flagstone paving turned glossy by the rain, a small
river in the gutter. My eyes closed. I reached back into my
memory, and tried to remember the sounds of boots on the
cobbles, the taste of the air washed clean by the storm. The
smell of the paint as my Mum stood in the shadow of the Guild
Hall, between two of the thick oak pillars that held it in the air,
with her easel and her paints, talking the whole time she
painted, neither the gossip, nor her swift brush strokes breaking
pace.

I tried to remember the feel of the fresh, cool, air on my face.

For a moment I almost succeeded. Then my side twinged and my eyes blinked open. I had a fresh dressing on. The graze was still tacky and scabbed. The bruises still tender to the touch. The outer rings were fading, but the nucleus of the bruises was as black and purple as ever.

I lay back on my bed and closed my eyes. Trying not to think of the dull throbbing pain in my side. I reached over and flicked the light off, as my head sank deep into the pillows. I steadied my breathing and waited for sleep to take me.

My phone danced on the bedside table as it let out a shrill ring. The screen cast a cone of light into the room, snapping me awake. I lifted myself to my elbows and grabbed the phone. The number was withheld. The clock said it was quarter past midnight. Too many thoughts blossomed in my head at once. Work. Lex. Cold callers telling me how much my accident was worth. Or Penny.

I hit the green icon. "Hello?"

There was a scratching, grinding sound on the far end of the line. A distant music, muffled as though it was in another room. Soft, slow, rasping breaths, like somebody struggling to make paper lungs inflate.

"Hello?" I repeated, expecting any moment to hear the rumbling gurgle of a phone caught in a pocket rubbing against something else. The same sound you hear when your ears fill with water. I hit the button to hang up. Nothing happened. I looked at the screen and jabbed at it as hard as I could. But the line stayed open, the call kept on. Something changed. The music ripped to a stop, like a needle being knocked from the record player.

The breathing ceased. There was near silence for a moment. Then a dry, deep, grinding laugh.

The line clicked dead.

I thumbed a control and called the phone company. Even at that time of night I was in a queue. When my call was answered a polite person on the far end gave me a number that I wrote on the back of an envelope. It was a land line with an area code I didn't recognise.

"Did you want it blocked sir?" The operative on the help desk asked. "If it was a prank, or nuisance call."

"Yes." I said. "Please. I would be grateful."

There were some keys being stroked then: "That is done. If it happens again we can help you report it to the appropriate authorities. Or you could try your local police station on a non-emergency line."

I thanked them as much as I could, hung up and lay back to a light, fitful sleep.

*

Monday I spent at work. I graded papers. I taught year seven about Germany in the depression. The bad old days of hunger, fear, politics gone wild and fighting on the street. The afternoon was better. Year nine are studying the ways people lived in the Middle Age. Much closer to my specialisms, the stuff my degree was based on. The stuff that still made little sparks of excitement dance in my chest. Then I stayed late grading papers and marking reports. Dissecting reports. Plucking them apart word by word, looking for the seeds of promise I could use to encourage them with.

Then when I got home I played music and I baked. I made a pile of washing up that I could not bear to look at, and I offered the oven no respite. I baked a tea loaf and a sweetly spiced cake with a layer of caramelised apples through the middle and more caramel sauce spread over the top to go sticky and gooey.

I ate late, when I caught track of time and went to sit in the living room with a bowl of reheated pasta, to channel hop on television and try not to think of anything. Trying not to let the sound of the rain outside remind me of how it echoed in the car, masking my heartbeat as Penny leaned closer, her lips brushing mine.

My phone rang. The number was withheld.

I put it to my ear and accepted the call.

"Hey." Penny said. She was surrounded by the snare drum beat of the rain. Under a plastic roof. A conservatory, seemed unlikely. A bus stop seemed more likely.

"Hey." I answered. "Are you okay?"

"Yeah. I'm waiting for a late bus. Not looking forwards to a walk home." She said.

"You need a lift anywhere?" I asked.

She made a lot of noises that did not quite become a word.

"Okay. I shouldn't have asked." I said quietly. "You need somebody to talk to a while?"

"Yeah." She said. "I tried not to, but I really think I do."

"Is it okay if I tell you that I'm glad you did?"

"You might not be." She said.

"I am right now." I paused. There might have been a chuckle on her end of the line. A grateful chuckle, clinging to what little joy I could offer. "I can't imagine not being glad to hear from you."

"So, I was in my kitchen earlier and I found an old pack of cards at the back of the drawer full of junk. Everybody has a drawer full of junk, and a tobacco tin full of crap. And everybody has a pack of cards. I tried playing patience, got bored, and it's much easier to play on the phone when you are on the bus. But I have the pack of cards, I have a King and a Queen, and I hear there is a game you can play with those two cards?"

"Only the King and Queen of Hearts." I said.

"If this is Trumps it will be a real short game." She said.

"It's a mystery game." I said. "Find the Queen of Spades, she can join in later."

"Okay. King of hearts. Queen of hearts. Queen of spades. Why a mystery game."

"Look at the King of hearts and tell me what you see." I said.

"A man. With a white beard. Dressed jolly. And one hand on his side. One is scratching behind his ear with a sword." Penny spoke gently and patiently.

"Sure?" I asked.

I could feel Penny glowering down the line. "No hang on. The angle is wrong. The cuffs are different."

"Right." I said.

"Oh. I see. If I put him next to the Queen, she is stabbing him in the back." Penny laughed a little. "The cuff matches hers. She is reaching behind him."

"It isn't always her." I said. "Sometimes it is the Jack, or one of the other kings. Sometimes the Queen of Spades. Like I said. It's a mystery game. One of a few you can play."

"Like?" Penny growled something. "The bus is here. I have to go."

"Sure." I paused. "You going to have a signal?"

"Subtle." She purred. "No. Don't come find me."

"Talk to me later?" I said. "Wake me up when you get home?"

"You don't want to do this." She said. "I don't want to do this."

"Then why call?" I said, gently. "If you need something, ask. Please. It would be-"

"I have to go." She said. "I'm sorry. Maybe soon."

She rang off.

*

"I can't be doing this Pickles." I said. "I can't be lying in bed wondering if a girl I barely know will want to call." I looked at the badger. "To tell me I'm not to talk to her."

Pickles remained silent.

"I have work tomorrow, and an evening thing with Lex." I rubbed my head. I was on the bed, staring at the ceiling. "I can't-"

My phone burst to life. I groaned and rolled onto my elbow, careful of my side. I picked up the phone. Another strange number, from the area code I didn't recognise. I cancelled the call. Before I put the phone down it was ringing again. I cancelled. On the third attempt I picked it up.

"Yes?" I said.

Distant music, muffled so I could barely make out the melody. Rasping breath.

I hit the cancel button.

The dry gurgle of a laugh. It grew louder and louder.

I jabbed at the cancel button.

The laugh howled like an animal. It twisted into a primordial scream of rage.

I flipped the phone over, and released the battery. It went dead.

I sat there breathing for a few seconds. I flicked on the lights and went downstairs. A few minutes later I had the sticky note with my reference on and a warm jumper on. I called the help desk from my land line, and left it a while before I put the battery back in the mobile. While I waited to be connected I fired up my laptop and started typing the numbers into the search engine.

"I can see the problem." The supervisor told me. "I can block that number too. In fact both are from a defunct switchboard, numbers that should be out of service."

"Is that possible?" I asked.

"On paper no. But in practice? It's an old hacker trick from the dial up days. I'm blocking all the numbers from that switchboard." The supervisor sighed. "It's a bit old fashioned, but some Hackitvists like that. Anybody who would want you harassed?"

"My ex-wife?"

"More likely you were chosen at random." He growled. "I'm keeping records for police too, if you want to inform them. I'll be sure they are in touch with you."

"Great. Thanks." I opened a few of the links from the search engine. "Can you tell me where the disused switchboard was?"

"I can't. The police may." He said.

I stared at my screen. "Bramling Bay hospital?"

"I can't say." He said.

"I couldn't hang up. It kind of jammed my line is that normal?" I said.

He paused.

"That should not be possible. It might be handset fault." He took on a sympathetic tone. "You didn't take your last upgrade. I can send you a new handset, and send you a new SIM with a new number. Newer model of what you have is a little more expensive every month, but that gives you a lot more data."

"Thanks. Whatever you can do." I said. When I finished speaking to him I called the police on the non-emergency line. I went through a few people, then I gave my name, my address, told my story, and gave them reference numbers for the phone company. I answered questions and registered the complaint. It all took time.

My mobile rang.

I felt pins and needles surround my heart as I reached for it. I set my jaw and glanced at the screen. A familiar mobile number. I answered.

"Hey." Penny said, brightly.

"Hi." I said.

"Wow. You sound awake." She didn't make it sound a good thing. "You okay?"

"Last couple of nights I've had some weird phone calls." I said. "Hopefully I have it sorted. I contacted the phone company. I contacted the Police."

"Oh." She sounded dour. Connections flashed together in my mind. Pieces of the puzzles fitted.

"I hate to ask this, and I really don't want to sound paranoid. But when you spoke about trouble that might find me, and your visits to somewhere with no signal, kind of mean I have to ask this..." I said. "Has some kind of hacktivist got it in for you?"

"It isn't like that." She said, softly. Her words tinged with guilt. "What happened?"

"There was music. Breathing. Background noise. I couldn't make out the tune, but it was familiar. Then laughter. Freaky laughter." I said.

"He didn't say anything? No message? No words?" She was urgent. Commanding.

"No." I said. "It's okay. Whoever it is, they were jumping off an old switchboard. Some kind of trick so they can use different numbers and get around a block. But I blocked the switchboard. I told the police. It's being dealt with. It's okay. He hasn't screwed with me. I'm only worried for you."

"He isn't messing with you. Not really. It's a way of getting at me." She sighed. "I'm home. Safe. I don't want you to worry about me." She thought a moment. "Okay. Listen. Speaking to you again was a mistake. Forget about me for a while. He won't bother you. He will be taking it out on me and..." Her voice shrank down and trailed away.

"And the more you make it sound that bad the less inclined I am going to be to leave you alone. Penny. If you won't talk about this, or if I can't help with this, I understand. But can I at least be the person who you let make you lunch or take you to films now and again. So the rest of the time the world is not quite so bad." I felt the past around me. Turning the shadows darker, and the air colder. I could feel the past looming over my shoulder making my hairs stand on end.

"That is stupid." She said. "You know this could be trouble for you."

"Yes. And I'm still asking if you want lunch sometime?" I swallowed.

"Why?" She whispered. "I don't...deserve this."

"Because when the world is darkest and coldest, knowing that somebody still wants to speak with you. Doesn't have to be a date, or anything. Just, I know what it is like to feel radioactive. To feel so bad you aren't even sure you are human any more." I paused. "whatever is going on in your world I can't know about. I can't help. But let me make you lunch. Please?"

She didn't say a word.

"My mobile number won't change for a few days. Think about it. Please." I said.

She didn't speak, and didn't ring off.

"When my number changes, want me to text you?" I said.

She let out a long sigh. "Thank you."

Her last words echoed a long time after the call ended. They were bitter sweet. They sounded of tears and of smiles, and they carried the echoes of words best left unsaid. I could barely hear them over the hammer of my heart and all the noise in my head. It was almost drowned out by the little voice screaming 'oh you SO like her' at me from the back of my mind in a voice that sounds like some of the words are underlined in red felt tip, and surrounded by love hearts with arrows through them.

I took the Masterpiece Deck, checked the doors were locked, set the alarms and made my way back up stairs.

I glanced at pickles as I sat down. "Don't say anything. whatever I want is not as important as what she needs. Okay?"

Pickles stared back at me. As I lay down I lifted pickles from the pillow and left him on my chest. I patted his head. "She doesn't need me to fancy her. She needs..." I frowned. "I think she just needs to know her troubles aren't her whole world. Does that make sense?" I lifted the badger and nodded its head. "See. Great minds think alike."

I set him aside on his pillow, turned my back on the cold side of the bed. I was never going to sleep right away. I practised shuffling the Major arcana. Sometimes with a trick to put them in order, sometimes to make them random. Eventually my mind settled, the noise and the static faded. I don't remember setting the cards aside. I don't know when I fell asleep. When I started to remember the hours I spent making the cards, copying the drawings, with Nan and with Mum watching me at the kitchen table. From the inside the memories were happy. In the dream I didn't miss them. I didn't feel the sting of their absence.

FIVE

Don't be mad. The words brushed the back of my neck. In the fog of half sleep, as the last tendrils of my dream kept hold of me the bed felt warm. I felt the mattress shifting under me as Jean rolled over and put a hand on my shoulder. I felt fingers on my shoulder. They were just words. Stupid. Angry. Spiteful. But words. I wouldn't...

"But you did say it." I said. The words shook me awake. I swallowed back the anger. The fury that sat in my chest like a cold, jagged rock. Digging into my lungs. I woke to a bed half cold. Half empty. "You did say it. You did mean it." I glanced at my phone over in the charging cradle. I still had fifteen minutes until my alarm went off. I closed my eyes, tried to think of eyes full of sympathy and a smile full of mischief. I let the anger melt away. "But the past done and forgiveness is easy."

It's forgetting which is difficult. We don't need ghosts to be haunted. The ghosts of the living followed me to the shower and left me with muscles knotted and braided with tension, and a neck so stiff I could use it as an anvil.

I spend the day shuffling around the school like a zombie. Sleepwalking through my classes, following the lesson plans like a script, and making best use of well-rehearsed lectures and exercises set out well in advance.

At break my phone rang. Lex.

"You remembered the thing tonight?" She said in a hurry, as I answered.

"Yeah." I leaned over my desk. "I have the caramel apple cake. And tea loaf. And my cards."

"You sound weird. Things good?" She asked.

"No." I groaned. "I didn't sleep much. There was this thing with phone calls the last few nights. I had to phone the company to get some blocked. They were hacking... something. And then call the police. Now my number is going to change and when my phone rings at night I don't know if it is Penny needing somebody to talk to, or if it is this... Person."

"Oh." Lex was lost for words. "Something you need to tell me?"

"I would love to, but I really don't know if I understand it right now. I..." The little sleep I had left me feeling ragged and exhausted. It only served to remind me how much I was missing. My head was full of fuzz and static. "I think it's baggage Penny brought with her."

"And telling you to run for the hills is pointless, I take it?" Lex asked.

"She doesn't act like she has anybody else." I said.

"Oh, so this is me setting a bad example?" She laughed. "Anything else?"

"I have to cover for an English lesson later. Do you know how hard it is for a history nut to read Shakespeare's historical plays, and not shout 'wrong' every five minutes?" I lowered my voice. "He made Macbeth the bad guy. And do not get me started on Julius Caesar."

"Those are beautiful works of poetry and drama." Lex said, as though I was a kicking a puppy.

"Sure." I agreed. "But you know how you scoff at doctors in movies?"

"Uh huh." She said. "Okay. I get the point. You up for tonight?"

"Absolutely." I said. "I think I need it."

She paused. "Birdie." She whispered my name. "Birdie, you sure about that? If you want to back out, I won't be upset. I'll collect the cakes and I'll... You know..."

"It's been a while since I did this." I felt myself wake up a little. "For a group. And a longer while since I saw any of your friends. It'll be nice."

"That's the point." She said, quietly. "They aren't just my friends."

"Right." I said. Jean's friends and Lex's friends are much the same. Put them in a Venn diagram and the middle ground is awfully crowded. "Sorry should I not come?"

She paused. She considered. "Yeah. Of course you should come. Just wanted to make sure you knew what it was. If you are out of shape, I don't want to put you somewhere terrible."

"Do they want me there?" I asked.

"Actually, yeah. I think they do." She said, brightly. "You know what. I said something stupid. I made this awkward. Birdie, I asked for the readings. So please, please, forget this conversation and come over. You are right. You need this."

*

I sat in the car, watching the house for three minutes before I made myself get out the door. I watched Janice and Dee strut their way up the steps and ring the bell. Lex has a hell of a house. A tall, Regency town house. The kind where the servants used to work downstairs, in the kitchen, now a wine cellar, and scullery (now a utility room), and the residents enjoyed the three floors above. I was parked under one of the oaks that lined the avenue, a little part of me dreaming of the day I could afford to even be seen at this end of town. With my cards in my bag, and the cakes loaded up in my arms, I fumbled with the fob to lock the car and darted across the road. At the top of the steps I held the stacked cakes in one arm, pinned with my chin while I groped for the doorbell.

"Hey." Lex shouted from somewhere beyond. "It will be Birdie. Can you get it?"

"Sure." A wholesome voice, with charm, sophistication and far too much money said. The door opened. Troy, the tall, handsome, devilish gym bunny opened the door and grinned at me from behind his shaven head and designer stubble. "Hey. Jack right?"

"Troy." I said, trying not to sound too panicked. I looked to the waif in the red dress standing beside him. The freckle faced woman whose face was always trying to resist the frown it fell too easily into. "Jo."

Troy took one of the cakes from, me to help me. He gave me a sympathetic look.

"Is Jean...?" I didn't quite manage to ask.

His eyes went flinty for a moment. Then he forced himself to smile. It was a little tepid. "No." He said with a shake of the head. "Jean is sitting this one out."

"Oh." I smiled. "Right. Sorry."

"Sorry?" Jo growled the word. "Wanker."

"What?" I felt my heart sink. "Sorry. Have I said or done..."

"Forget it." Troy patted my shoulder. "Go cut up the cakes. I am sure the girls will love to see you." He ushered me down towards the kitchen, where it sounded like more wine was being shared than tea or coffee. Laughter too. I set the cakes on the side and Lex gave me a huge smile. Three sizes too big for her face.

"Caramel apple?" She asked.

I nodded.

"You are a godsend." She grinned.

"Lex." I felt some scowls burning into me as Jo started to whisper away. "I just saw Troy and asked if Jean was here and I think I just-"

"It's fine." Lex forced her smile to stay in place. "Just throw some cash in the bucket and nobody will remember after two wines and your card tricks." She reached over to the kitchen worktop and shook a bucket full of change, decorated with the charity logo. "Okay ladies. The cakes are both free and to die for. But some sterling gets your fortune read. No need to cross his palm with silver, just fill my bucket with fivers"

There were some cat calls.

"What do we get for a tenner?" A happy looking woman I didn't know asked loudly.

"You get to call him a tosser. For twenty quid you get to slap the little f-" Jo answered.

"Jo." Troy hissed the word sharply.

"What?" Jo tried to whisper back, but her whisper had always been the loudest in Kent. Troy grabbed her arm and dragged her up the stairs. There were wolf whistles following him. Lex passed me a knife.

"Everybody gets a bit of both cakes." She said with forced brightness. "Please."

I nodded and looked at the ladies with a smile as I got the plates from her cupboard and cut the cake. Most the familiar faces broke into welcoming smiles. I got pats on the arm and told I had been away too long, or that I was looking better. Everybody else told me how nice the cakes looked, or asked who I was.

I put some slices of the cakes on a plate with some napkins and stepped out into the hall with my bag. Lex was coming back the other way, a frown on her face. She started when she saw me.

"Where did you want me?" I asked.

She pointed up to the dining room. "Use the table. I will get a few of the girls to go up at a time so you can talk them through what you do, then give them a reading?" She took the biggest slice of the apple cake on a napkin. Then she thought better and took the plate. "I'll let Jo and Troy find these when they are done bickering."

"What did I do?" I asked.

"Nothing. You know Jo. She has to find a reason to say something dumb at any party."

"She does?" I was not so sure.

"Forget it." Lex grinned. "Everybody else has." She kissed my cheek. "Go get ready. I will love you forever for this mate."

I let her take the plate from me and I hurried upstairs. As I approached the dining room I could hear voices drifting across the hall. The door to the front room was slightly ajar, with two figures moving around just inside.

"Not at all?" Jo asked, quiet and subdued all of a sudden.

"Not a word." Troy said, as I set a doorstop to hold the dining room door open, set my silk sheet over one end of the table and started to shuffle the Major Arcana deck.

"Jesus." Jo whispered, loudly. I had some prop coins to weigh down the sheet, and a candle for mood. I put the candle on a place matt and adjusted the lights.

"Jean asked him not to know." Troy said. I froze. I started trying to listen. He continued after a moment to draw breath. "She wanted a clean break from him, and he... Well... He had his own problems. If he's at arm's length, he won't rush over to see her, she can be happy knowing they both came through it all. Before this."

"Fuck." Jo suddenly was not whispering. She was standing in one door, staring right through the other at me. I pretended not to notice, shuffling my cards. I glanced up.

"Oh. Sorry. There's cake downstairs for you." I said, fixing a poker look on my face.

"Jack." Troy looked at me. "Did you..?"

"If it was anything I was meant to hear, you would have told me." I said as kindly as I could manage. "Whatever I did or said, I'm sorry. I didn't mean to upset you Jo. Can I do anything to prove that?"

"No." Jo sounded like a mouse all of a sudden. Small and squeaky. "My bad. I misheard you mate. Sorry. You know how it can be right?"

"Oh." I nodded. "I think so. Sorry."

Troy grinned. "Cool. So these are the magic cards?" He stepped into the dining room as Lex showed the first three game girls to the table. I waved for him to sit down and dug a ten pound note from my pocket.

"For the bucket." I said to Lex. "Troy can have a reading."

Lex recognised the olive branch and took the money with a little laugh. For a moment she gave me the same smile she always used to. For a second we might have twelve years old again, on a Saturday afternoon where we had nothing better to do than read her fortune. "Well, try to make him lucky. He's in the lottery syndicate."

I grinned at her joke. Everybody else made polite laughing noises.

I spread the cards so everybody could see them. Explained a little about them and the process I use. I explained it is non-standard, passed down through my family, and gave a little talk on how and why the cards came to be used for magic instead of games. I added a few tricks into the mix by sleight of hand, making the Sun become the Moon, and the Emperor become a Fool.

I handed the deck to Troy.

"Sorry. I can be a bit tricky. Probably better you shuffle for yourself or I might be tempted to tamper with the fates." I said it in the slightly dramatic voice I use for performance. "And besides, there is something special about taking fates into your own hands."

"Absolutely the way I want it." Troy said, obviously game. He shuffled the deck like it was poker night. He set out the seven cards as I showed him.

If they felt like family, I would be able to feel bad Birdie.

I blinked. The words hissed against my ear. For a second I could feel the ragged, sobbing breaths of the fight on my cheek. I blinked the memory away. I could feel the others looking at me. The stray fragment of one of the worst nights of my life was gone. A mote of dust carried in the air.

I reached over and turned the cards over.

If they felt like family I might lay awake and worry for them. Instead of wishing they would hurry up and die so you could just stop moping like a-

My eyes closed. I clenched my fist.

"Are you okay?" One of the women asked.

"The fates," I said, hoping they would think it was part of the act, "like to tell us a story. This," I held up my left hand, "is how the world impacts us." I clenched my other fist. "This is our impact on the world around us." I put a hand on my heart. "Our nature." I put a hand to my head. "Our intentions." I pointed to the cards. "Head. Heart. Left hand and right hand."

Everybody nodded.

"So Troy, your head, the way you think has the Lovers card. That means your judgement is based on love, relationships, choices and seeking harmony." I said.

"Great for us." One of the women said. "Not quite so good as a Solicitor."

"I think it makes me a good lawyer." He said. "I wish a few more clients had some harmony in their thoughts."

"Your heart is your nature. They are what comes to you without thinking. They are what are left in the moments you don't think. The Hermit represents introspection, inner reflection and contemplation. But also self-sufficiency. While the Hierophant is all about conformity, society, the greater good of the people." I smiled. "So even when you are the lone voice in the wilderness you will stand for the values you believe make society work."

There were appreciative mumblings around the group.

"Your left hand, the influence the world has upon you is represented by..." I looked at the cards. "The Tower and the Hanged Man. The tower is change. Sudden and unexpected change. Not always disaster, but always an upheaval and a complete change. The Hanged Man is something suspended or sacrificed." I swallowed. For a second everything felt too light, as though gravity was playing tricks on me. Troy was staring at me, something intense in his eyes. "I do not think it is unreasonable to assume that a Solicitor, one working in criminal law, is often thrown into unpredictable circumstances, and expected to sacrifice time and effort for his work."

One of the women started to whisper something to her neighbour. She got a nudge from an elbow. I chose to ignore it.

"The right hand, your impact upon the world balances the scale however. The Star and the Sun are both the brightest of cards. The sun brings warmth and joy, the star brings hope and serenity. Together they burn brightest. Even in the darkest times, even when tested, you will guide others to goodness."

Do you want to know who I lay awake at night and think about? It isn't them is it?

I blinked against the memory.

"A good man." I said. "Basically you are a good man."

"Well we didn't need cards to tell us that." The woman next to him gave him a playful hug.

Troy had two fingers. He was tapping the hanged man.

"It is something we have to suspend or to sacrifice. But it also brings a change of perspective. A new way of seeing the world. The tower may not always be a change for the worse. But it will be a difficult change. The world does not make your path easy at times, but it is a path you are well armed for."

"Yes." He said, quietly. "There have to be dark times for me to burn brightest? Isn't that what they say?"

"Perhaps. Or perhaps you are just better prepared to face the darkness, knowing you can carry a little of the light with you." I said.

He nodded. "Thank you Birdie." He shuffled the cards together. "That is good to know."

He handed the deck to the woman beside her. She concentrated hard on shuffling them, then drew her seven. I gave her a smile, feeling my way into the groove. I looked at the Wheel card in the head position. I looked up to the woman who was dressed in clothes that were flattering without flaunting, loose and comfortable. She toyed with an engagement or a wedding ring she was not quite used to yet.

"The Wheel is all about being lucky isn't it?" She asked.

"Yes. But it is also about life cycles." I watched her eyes. Her lips opening a little. Her skin flushing. "And turning points." I said, watching her react again. "Are congratulations in order yet, or are you still trying to be a mother?"

"No." The woman shook her head. "No. You git." She laughed a little. "We haven't told anybody yet!"

One of the other women threw her arms around her, laughing loudly and congratulating her.

"Shh!" The woman laughed. "None of you are meant to know!"

"Still trying then." I said, miming a zip of my lips. I gave her my best smile. "Let's look at your heart shall we?" I paused. "I would just like to point out to those of you drinking wine, the card has other meanings, so if it crops up again it might not be quite the same message."

I closed my eyes. No more whispers in my mind. I moved on to the next cards.

*

Most of the first group left. Only Troy remained sat perfectly still. He was trying to look cheery, trying to be the stand-up guy. He let the others stand, leaning on the table.

"Birdie." He said. "What you heard..."

"Isn't my business." I said softly. The words felt barbed. They went against my every instinct. "Until she asks me. But if there is ever anything-"

"She knows." He patted my shoulder. "I know. But don't take this the wrong way, but I hope I never have to. So just don't ask."

I said nothing. I felt myself nod as though I was not actually in my body. "Lex said that Jean didn't know how bad things were for me. That if she saw me it would open wounds, with guilt and... I won't do that. She needs to move on right? When she needs to ask, she can ask. Anything. I..."

"Fair enough." Troy said, breaking the awkward pause. He nodded. He had more to say, but was relieved to have a dodge. He took it and shook my hand. "I'll give her your love, tell her you are doing okay. Nothing too fancy. I won't make it sound like you are gloating."

He walked out. There was a few minutes before Lex would show the next group in. I stood at the window. I took my phone out and checked it. Then I shuffled the deck, hoping to lose myself in the cards, to keep the fragments of stray memories at bay. I dealt myself a pair of cards.

Death and the Devil were dancing again.

I flicked the cards back to deck and started to shuffle them again. I held the deck to my lips. "Stop trying to scare me." I whispered. "Please."

The door swung open. Lex was stood there with a coffee for me. A sliver of tea loaf. The next group of women behind her.

"Cards behaving themselves?" She asked, sitting behind me.

I gave her a tired look. "I've just been looking too hard for patterns in the random."

"You ready?" She asked, putting a hand on my shoulder and watching me shuffle. She stayed there as I went through the readings, her chin resting on her palms, just like a kid. Just like the old days. She even had the same smile on her lips.

The one that always sang 'I know something you don't know.' The one that was always full of secrets.

SIX

I got home, stood in the shower, and then fell face first into the bed. I glanced over at Pickles and dropped into a deep sleep before I could say a word. Almost instantly my alarm clock sounded. I opened my eyes. Suddenly it was six in the morning and my side felt like it was being attacked by a pillar drill. I showered and changed my dressing. The graze was still scabbed. The bruises still livid, shrinking and congealing to a shape. If I had an extra finger it might have been a hand print.

"What the hell did I do to myself?" I muttered. I sprayed it clean and applied a dressing.

The postman buzzed on the doorbell. He swapped me a new phone and new SIM card for an autograph on his PDA. I added it to my satchel, and tried to work out how to swap my contacts between the phones, wirelessly.

I grabbed breakfast to go, and was at work early enough to set up the new phone, text most my contacts with the new number, and to have my laptop jacked in to the projector and running through the slide shows for the day. I had my notes organised. I had everything ready. I met my year eleven class with a smile. None of the class shared it.

The morning classes flew past. I got year eleven discussing the history of Vaccination. After the morning break year nine were discussing the early years of the Nazi party and how they cemented power.

At lunch the department secretary poked her head around my door. I was eating lunch al-desko, with a pile of papers to be marked and a plastic container full of salad. She smiled at me. It was a hollow smile. The kind you use when you really aren't sure what to do with your face. When you are afraid of flying and the plane just entered a storm, for example.

"Mister Bird." She met my eyes. "You have a call."

"I do?" I looked at my mobile.

"Misses Bird." She said.

I blinked. "Jean?"

"She sounds pretty scared. Pretty messed up." The secretary said.

I nodded and hurried to the office and took the phone I was being offered.

"Hello." I said.

"Jack." Jean whispered the word. Then she laughed a terrified relief. "Oh thank God Jack."

"Jean. What's wrong? Where are you?" I was trying my best to sound calm.

"I'm in hospital. I... I can't remember coming here." Her voice was wavering. "I tried home, and I tried your mobile and... And... Please come get me."

"Where are you?" I asked.

"Hospital. I'm in..." She looked around, breathing hard.

"Miss Webb?" Another voice on the end of the phone. It was a long time since I heard her maiden name being used. It was taking time to get used to. "Miss Webb, I think you need to come back to bed."

"No." Jean sounded dazed, almost dreamy, but her voice was quivering with fear and confusion. "I mean yes. But I'm Mrs Bird. See?"

I choked. It is weird how some words can only sound right with an inflection? For ten years Jean had a way of saying 'See?' that she only ever used when she held up her ring finger, for somebody to inspect.

There were six long, slow, torturous seconds in which she just breathed.

"But.. But..."

"Jean, are you okay?" I asked.

"They took my ring." She whispered.

"Easy now Miss Webb." The voice was silky smooth and full of kindness. "Let's get you back to bed. Mister Johan will be here later."

"Mister Johan?" Jean brightened at the sound of the name, but was still confused.

"Troy." I said gently. "Troy will be there to look after you."

There was something I couldn't hear. Jean being ushered away.

"Hello?" The voice on the far end of the phone said.

"Who is this?" I asked.

"Doctor Morgan. Who am I speaking to?"

"Jack Bird." I said. "Jean's husband. Ex-husband. Where are you?"

There was a pause.

"I'm sorry." His voice became forced. "I can't share patient details without consent."

"She said she was in hospital, and she sounded... What's wrong?" I tried to keep my temper.

"I am sorry." Morgan said, firmly. "But I can not share patient details."

"Because of the divorce? Because she cut me off?"

"I'm sorry." He repeated. "But she made certain requests while she was more...lucid."

The line went dead.

I dug out my phone and rang Troy. His line was engaged. I could imagine Doctor Morgan on the phone to him. 'Oh hello. I'm afraid I found Jean on the phone. You know the guy nobody was meant to tell? Sorry about that.'

I tried again. He blocked me and it went to voice mail. "Hi Troy. I just had a call from Jean. She said she was in hospital and I have to be honest, I am scared to hell by what I heard. So... You know what. Ring me back. Now."

I paced in circles.

"Is something wrong?" The secretary asked.

I nodded.

"Personal emergency?" She asked.

"I don't know." I flicked through my contacts to Lex and hit dial. No response. The number is unavailable. She works in a hospital. Of course it is. I called her switchboard number.

"Kensington." She answered.

"Lex." I tried to sound light. "Hi. I just had a call from Jean."

There was a pause. "What did she say?"

"That she's in hospital. Why is she in hospital? Is this what I'm not meant to know? To ask?" I felt hot tears burning my cheeks and stinging my eyes. "What's going on?"

"She rang you?" Lex spoke in a tone that cut through everything.

"Yes." I said.

"And?"

"She acted like she didn't know we were divorced. Like a few years had not happened." I said quietly. "And she seemed pretty freaked out that her husband was not with her."

"Right." Lex said. "So if you swan in there, no ring on your finger, looking like you look, what the hell is she going to think?"

"Lex. Where is she?" I said.

"You can't go. She didn't want that. She left instructions. She made herself absolutely clear to me and to Troy. You can't. You aren't even meant to know." She groaned.

"So I start ringing every hospital in the country asking for Doctor Morgan? I'm guessing London. How many can there be? I mean, can I at least send flowers, or a care package, or something?"

"Okay." Lex let out a long slow breath. "I need to talk to Troy. Don't rush there. If you turn up asking for her at reception then security will get involved. Not unless we sign off on it first."

"Is she at Bramling Bay?" I asked.

"No." She missed a beat. "Where did you hear that name?"

"Doesn't matter. Where is she?" I asked.

"Queen Street." Lex said as calmly as she could manage.

"Queen Street?" I felt the world falling apart around me.

"Yeah. The Neurology and Neurosurgery ward."

"Neurology and Neurosurgery? Like brain stuff?"

"Yeah." Lex said gently. "Like brain stuff."

The phone fell away from my ear. My hands were dead weights at my side. The world tumbled past on the wrong axis. I had to steady myself against the desk. Lex had to hang up and ring me back to get me to talk to her.

"Birdie?" Lex said.

"Yeah."

"Listen." She spoke softly and quietly. "She wanted to protect you from this. But..." She sighed. "But now you know. Let me talk to Troy. Don't rush up there. Just let me talk to Troy."

"Yeah." I said in a daze.

"You okay?" Lex asked. I didn't answer. I was throwing up into a waste paper bin. Then I sat in my class with a cup of tea and eyes glazed over. I think I threw up again before somebody decided it was a sick day and I was sent home.

*

Friday evening I got the train up to London with Lex. We were fighting against the tide of commuters heading the other way. Evacuating the city for the weekend. She held my arm the whole way. I was staring out the window, watching the fields give way to the sprawl of the urban. As we were approaching the husk of Battersea power station, with Canary Wharf on the skyline, my phone started to ring.

"Hello?" I said, with it pressed to my ear.

"Hey." Penny said. "So... Had any more trouble?"

"Not the kind you mean." I said.

"What's wrong?" The giggles were gone from her voice in an instant.

"My ex is ill. I'm heading into London to see her." I said. "It's serious."

"Crap. Sorry. You going to be okay?" She asked.

"Yeah. I think so." I said. "Thanks for asking. You okay?"

"Yeah. Same as always." She didn't make that sound too convincing. "So. You need to talk about it later?"

"Can I ring you?"

"Oh." She let out a sigh. "That might be awkward."

"I think I know where you will be if you don't answer."

"Yeah." She laughed. "Bring food?"

"Always." I promised. "Might only be a take out."

"Worked last time." She paused. "Take care of yourself won't you?"

"I'll speak to you later. One way or another." I said.

Lex watched me hang up. "Still seeing the troubled one?"

"She didn't sound too troubled." I said.

"Well, I think we have enough of our own right now." She patted my leg. "Come on." She took my hand and walked me to the doors of the carriage, so we could watch Victoria station rolling out to meet us.

A few tube stations later we were at the big building of old stone and modern glass, ducking into a visitor's reception and asking if we could see Jean. Computer screens were checked, and a nurse consulted before we were told we could go ahead. Lex hooked her arm through mine and clenched my hand in a tight grip as we followed the signs to the elevator, ascending to the upper floors, where the air tasted of disinfectant and smelt of vinegar.

Doctor Morgan was a petite man, with thinning hair, thick glasses and bold shirts. He shook my hand firmly.

"How much do you understand about her situation?" Morgan asked. He gave Lex a smile.

"Lex told me Jean has a tumour, a growth, in her brain." I said. "It's been there a while?"

"A few years, we think." He said, gently. "Benign for much of the time, then, we think perhaps some of the earliest symptoms were masked. You, of course know that times were turbulent. It is possible some of the warning signs were put down to stress, or to the result of her emotional state." He paused. "We can-not say for sure. But she believes she acted out of character a few times."

Do you want to know who I lay awake and think about? It isn't them?

"Yes." I said. "So... I... Left her when she was ill? Because she was ill?"

"I can-not say that. Only that perhaps this is the reason warning signs were missed." He tried to look kind. "For several months we have treated it chemically. But recently she has been, well, on the phone to you she was confused. That morning she knew where she was and why, that afternoon she was three or four years in the past. Yet she retained memories. She knew who her current partner was, when we told her she was divorced she understood. But she had to try to remember."

I nodded. "What did this?"

"We do not know." Morgan sighed. "A quirk of the genetic lottery perhaps?" He showed me to one of the doors. "I think seeing you will help. Now she is ready."

"If I can help at all." I said, quietly.

Alex opened the door to one of the rooms. There was a bed, a table with a vase of flowers. Some chairs, one of which was occupied by Troy. And laying in the bed, her shaven head bandaged beneath a bandanna, was a skeleton in a bag of flesh who looked a lot like the woman I once loved utterly and completely.

Every dark wish and bitter thought that I had muttered in the dead of night, when anger and loss had kept me awake was a whiplash across my heart. Every second I had not been here was a hell that would be waiting for one day.

She glanced up, her eyes focussing on mine.

"Jean." I said, softly.

"Birdie." Jean gripped Troy's hand in both of hers, the pipes from her drip hanging from her wrist. "I..." She look confused.

"You rang him remember." Troy said. "At the school. Gave the poor man a fright."

"Are you here to take me home?" Jean asked quietly. She screwed up her face. "Please? I don't know if I like it here."

"I can't take you home yet." I set my bag down and bent over to kiss her forehead. She tried to meet my lips with hers, but I planted the kiss above her eye and stood back. "They need to take care of you a little longer before they can send you home with Troy."

"Troy." She blinked and looked at the guy holding her hand. Her lips parted to a big smile.

"Hey." Troy said, squeezing her fingers.

"Sorry." She laughed, faintly. "I sometimes... I should never forget you."

"Anything that makes you happy." He said.

"I thought..." She trailed off. "It doesn't matter. For now." She looked at me. "What happened to you Jack? You look terrible."

"Guy who makes cakes every week should never look that thin." Lex agreed, stooping to give Jean a kiss. "He's fine. A few rough nights and a busy time at the school."

"I brought you something." I dug in my bag, producing one battered looking badger stuffed with dried beans. I held Pickles up and made him wave.

"Oh God." Jean laughed. "Pickles." She held out her hands for him. I let him go and felt a little tug on my heart as she buried his snout on her chest and clamped her arms around him. She held him close. "Did you bring cakes and cards?"

"No. Sorry." Damn it, why did I not bring those? "I wasn't sure you would want that."

"S'okay." She gave Pickles an Eskimo kiss. "You did fine." She patted the bed beside her and waited for me to sit. "You look terrible."

"I know." I said.

"I..." She looked over at Troy. "Could I have a minute? With Birdie?" She glanced to Lex too. "I think there is stuff I need to say."

"You sure you want this?" Troy said, gently.

"I said what I said back when this was going to be easy. A few chemical sessions and some luck. Now they want to cut me open and zap me, I think the rules changed a little." She gripped his hands for strength. "I think I need to say some stuff to my husband in case I don't get another chance."

Troy looked at me.

"He can stay." I said.

"No." Jean shook her head. "No he can't. Please."

"Okay." Troy unpeeled himself from her. "Whatever makes you happy."

They stepped outside and closed the doors.

"I'm sorry." I said. "For everything."

She reached up and stroked my cheek. "What the hell happened to you?"

"I fell to pieces a little. I'm better. I'm doing good. I think I started dating again, but it's all a little complicated." I said. "Jeany, why would you not tell me about this?"

"Because you would rush up here, offer to do anything I bloody asked, and..." She closed her eyes. "And still act like you love me. Not in love with me. I burned that bridge and bombed the ashes. But look at you. Look at us? After all I did?"

"We did." I said. "We both made mistakes. We both fell out of love. We argued. It's not a tally. It's not about who owes the other a kindness. I'm sorry I..."

"They weren't all mistakes." She said, quietly.

I sat in silence, waiting for the sting to pass.

"I'm sorry." She whispered. "But it was easier to live with the stuff I didn't mean if I could believe you deserved it. All I had to do was believe you meant everything the way it sounded, to pretend not to know how you would be saying it."

I sat quietly. I patted her hand. "You did what you needed to do. To cope. You never meant to hurt anybody. I already told you that it's all forgiven."

She was trying to lay back down. I adjusted her pillows and put Pickles beside her.

"You didn't even notice I was gone for-"

"Two days." She said. "The rest was just to... I don't know... Punish you. I'm sorry."

Her confession made my heart stop, my lungs empty. I felt my blood stop flowing and start pooling, my arms turn to stone. My head turning light. The world growing cold, dark, silent around me. Anger burned in my chest, the betrayal stabbing at me.

I tried to look beyond it.

"I know you are." I sighed. "Me too. I've got more than enough to be sorry for. I'll go get the others."

"Jack." The tone of her voice stopped me before I stood. She looked over at me. "I lost your Mum and your Nan in a year. You may have issued the papers, but I couldn't lose you. I had to push. I had always been pushing." She looked at me. "I had to."

Do you want to know who I lay awake and think about?

The memory slipped into my mind. I tried to bury it. Forgiven, forgotten, and left behind long ago.

"Jack?" Her voice was muffled, distant, distorted.

I shook my head. I was over this.

"Birdie?"

"Yeah. You pushed. Before London. Forgiven, forgotten, and trying to decide what cake you get when you come out the other side." I stepped away. "You're looking tired. I'd better let that boyfriend of yours make the most of this." I gave her all the warmth I had as I walked away.

"Jack."

I looked back from the door.

"Don't send the cake up with Lex." Her voice was muffled by the badger. "I... The times I forget. The times I forget I pushed you. They're... I don't want to ever lose Troy, but... they make me feel safe. I want to feel safe. I am sorry. For so much."

"Me too." I repeated.

I forced myself to smile, until I was out the door. Then as I stumbled through the corridor I found a bench to lean on. I closed my eyes and counted to twenty.

"You okay?" Lex asked.

"Jack?" Troy asked.

"Just need some air." I said. My body was still heavy, my lungs were full of stones. I waited for the room to stop spinning around me.

SEVEN

We were on the train home, sat side by side. We brought coffees at the station and I sent a message to Penny, letting her know we were on the way home. Lex curled up against me, put an arm around me.

"You okay?" She asked.

I nodded.

"Want to talk about it?" Lex asked.

"When I thought she hadn't noticed I was gone that first week, it was brutal, but it was...I don't know. Innocent in a way. Unintended." I frowned. "But she knew after two days. She said she punished me."

"For what?" Lex asked.

I shrugged. "We argued the night before I left. For what was said then."

"What about?" Lex lifted herself from me to get a better look.

"It doesn't matter. How few friends we had in London? How long I spent commuting, and how much harder I should have looked for a job? How many nights I spent marking extra exams for a little more cash?" I shrugged. "What matters is how she ended it. The trump card she could play that ended an argument without resolution. It doesn't matter what the argument was, she could just tell that I was bullying her in revenge for something she said back home. Proper home. Not the flat. After Nan was in the accident. While Mum was..." I swallowed. "There were those few days when both of them were in hospital, one in Ashford, one in Margate."

Lex put her hand on mine.

"She wanted them to hurry up and die. They weren't her family." I whispered. "And any time we argued, she could remind me how mad I was at that. Say that was the reason I was being so unreasonable. It would always hit me like a sledgehammer to the happy sacks. I... I couldn't face that argument again. I would let her have whatever victory she wanted, and go to walk it off, or go to sleep in another room. I would just fold."

"She never told me." Lex whispered. "You never told me."

"Now maybe we know why she just pulled that out of nowhere." I said, closing my eyes. "Forgiving is easy. I keep trying to forget, but..."

"You sure you want to see your friend tonight?" She put a hand on my knee. "I have beer. DVDs. A spare bed. You can come forget everything if you want."

I smiled. "Sorry."

"Right." She picked up her coffee and toasted mine. "Go find another way to forget."

*

I drove down into the car park and headed for the isolated corner. Penny was sat under one of the trees, using the borrowed waterproof coat as a blanket, reading a beaten old paperback by the light of a torch she wore on her head like a miner. She glanced up as I parked and hurried to mark her page with a paper clip. She scooped up her coat and climbed in the car.

"Hey." She said.

"Hey." I agreed.

"You came?" She smiled.

"I wanted to see you." I said.

"With everything?" She said.

"I make you smile. I wanted to see somebody I could make smile." I handed her the bag of food. "It is becoming something of a novelty. To be the good thing in your life."

"Which tells you all you need to know about the rest of my life." She put the food aside and shuffled closer, toying with her hair.

"How about your life?" I said. "The stuff I'm not allowed to ask?"

"Don't matter right now." She took a pouch of fries from the bag on the central console. With her other hand she reached up and stroked my hair. "If I let them matter I am going to worry I can't do this to you and run away."

"Do what to me?" I said.

"Fall for you. Knowing what will follow me." She said.

"Maybe if trouble finds us both it will be easier?" I looked at her.

"No." She smiled. "Just easier to forget when it isn't here." She banished the doubts and the worries from her face. Suddenly, and I'm not sure how it happened, we were talking about movies, and books, while eating. I pretended not to notice how often she was looking at the clock over on the store. When she finished eating we ended up curled together. She shuffled against me, stroked my leg, and rested her head on my shoulder.

When Radio Four gave way to the World Service she put her phone back on.

"Want to go home?" I asked.

She looked at me. Shook her head. "I guess I have to."

"Or to mine?"

She paused. She smiled. "That would be a real bad idea right now."

"That's okay." I smiled. "I like this. For what it's worth. I like this."

"This is all it can be for now." She said, getting comfy. "Sorry."

"Sorry?" I squeezed her a little. "No. You don't get to be sorry for something I am thanking you for."

She flushed and toyed with her hair. "You really don't want to thank me."

"I do." I said. "Not in the way it might sound. Actual thanks."

She laughed. "I know what you meant. And you are welcome. You want the hell that comes with me, you are very welcome to whatever this is."

"I think the technical term for this is...nice." I said.

"Friend cuddles." She said. "Fruddles?" She smiled. "But nice works. Nice is true." She lifted herself off me. "Drive me home?"

I nodded and started the engine. "Look. If you ever need to stay at mine, I have a spare room and no fruddles or anything else would be expected. I know a good lawyer if it helps."

"You are the sweetest." She kissed me. "But there is somebody at home I really need to go look after. Sorry. It isn't about me or you. It's not that kind of trouble."

I nodded. We drove in silence. At the end of her road she made me pull over.

"So he doesn't see you." She said.

"Who?" I asked.

"And so he doesn't see this." She leaned over and kissed me. It started as a peck on the lips, but lingered and became hungrier, more intense and desperate. As she leaned back I followed her, caught in her flurry of kisses. My fingers found her hair, then the nape of her neck. Hers found my thighs, then my side. She drew me as close as we dared. As she parted from me my fingers brushed her cheek.

She smiled, holding up her hand for me to kiss. "Good night."

"See you soon?" I asked.

She nodded. "And thanks. So many thanks." She kissed my cheek.

I watched her walking away, down the street, her head rocked back to look at the stars. I watched as she paused at her gate. Hovering. Her feet dragging. Her steps growing reluctant. Lights in her house flicked on. They cast her in a golden light. As she approached, the front door opened. But I couldn't see anybody in there.

She looked back for a moment, then lowered her head and stepped into her house.

The door closed behind her, and all the lights went out.

*

I slept until late on Saturday morning with a lurch. I tumbled from my bed and hit the solid wooden floor with a jolt. I landed on my side, with the scabby bruise taking the brunt of the impact. My scream echoed through the bedroom. The pain that echoed through my body was all consuming. Lights flashed behind my eyes as everything turned red.

I dragged myself up. The scabs on my side had torn away, the graze had split into a jagged cut. Blood was seeping through my shirt, in a stain. I lurched to bathroom and pulled open the medicine cabinet in search of a dressing and some painkillers.

Something moved in the corner of my eye. I glanced around, seeing an empty bathroom. I walked back to the bed and looked at the mess I had made of my covers rolling around. On half the bed at least. Well, one little mystery seemed to be solved. If I wanted to avoid future bruises I needed a lower bed or softer floor.

I stumbled down the stairs and turned off the alarm. As I walked towards the kitchen the box beeped. I doubled back and disarmed it again. I held up a finger. "Behave."

As I stepped away the box beeped again. I doubled back and cancelled it. I rummaged in the drawers and found my multi-tool. I popped the cover from the box and checked the connections were all pressed down into place. I pushed the cover back on. "Before you beep one more time you should know they send me catalogues with the new systems. Surprisingly cheap."

It seemed to take the hint. I stared bleary eyed at the clock and went into the kitchen. I set the oven to heat up. I found my favourite bowl and started digging flour, butter, sugar, and the bottle of milk that did not smell like it was about to go for a walk. I set the food processor to mix them into muffin, with a sprinkle of baking soda. Some rummaging provided raspberries and a bar of white chocolate. I took my frustrations out on the chocolate with a toffee hammer, then its fragments and the raspberries went in the mixer.

The phone rang. I glanced over.

"Hey." Lex said, with forced brightness. "You okay?"

"Ugh." I said.

"Is that an emotional caveman voice, or a bruised caveman voice?"

"I fell out of bed again. And yes, I am sure that is what happened." I said. "I haven't eaten yet. In about twenty minutes I am going to have muffins and coffee ready if you want brunch, or elevenses, or something?"

There was a pause. "How are you holding up?"

I made the "Ugh" noise again.

"Twenty minutes." Lex promised.

"Lex. You okay?" I said.

"What you told me on the train. Was it true Birdie?"

"Yes." I sighed. "Sorry."

"Then no." Her tone softened. "No I am not happy those words were said. I keep telling myself it is not her, but something in her head. Some alien intruder who will be blasted. But those words were said, and they hurt, and..."

"And you are coming over for coffee and cakes, and this afternoon we are going to the farmers market and getting something to make for dinner. Okay?"

"I'll see you in twenty." She said, hanging up.

The alarm beeped. I walked over to the control box and pressed the cancel button. I paused. There was something... I turned to look at the big mirror. For a second I had thought there had been something about the light. The shadow. The shapes in the corner of my eye. I froze, ancient, primordial instincts holding me. I slowed my breathing.

"Is somebody there?" I asked, knowing how foolish those words sounded.

There was silence.

I looked up at the stairs. "Is somebody up there?"

By which I meant: 'If you broke into my house I know you are there.' I ducked into the living room cupboard and found the cricket bat, before I marched upstairs and searched every room. Nobody there. Nothing stirring.

Nothing, but the worst parts of my mind. I tossed the cricket bat onto the spare bed and grabbed my head. I shook it as though trying to get rid of all the clutter, the noise, the worries. It was all still. I walked back down to the kitchen and set the muffins to cook. I set the timer and opened some windows. I filled the coffee machine with the good coffee and I channel hopped on the radio.

Lex rang my doorbell fifteen minutes later. She was dressed in a casual shirt, jeans. She always found it so easy to look beautiful without trying. It was all about the smile. That morning it was gone. It was the first time in thirty years she hadn't smiled when I saw her. All the strength, all the support, all the love she had shown on the train was gone.

"You were asking me over, because you didn't want to be alone?" I said, realising I was indeed an arse of colossal proportions. "Oh God I am so sorry."

She nodded and stepped into the hall. I wrapped her into a cuddle and buried her head in my shoulder. I felt the muscles of her jaw and cheek twitching as she refused to cry. For a while we just stood there. She didn't say anything. She didn't need to. I ran my fingers down her hair.

"I am so, so, so, sorry." I whispered. "I should have known."

"It's okay." She tried to laugh. "I didn't even know what I wanted."

I nodded. "Even so..."

"Just be here now." She said. "Idiot."

She gripped me in the hug real tight. It hurt my side so bad, but I said nothing, I did nothing, I let her feel safe, until the timer on the oven went off. Then I took her hand and guided her to the kitchen. I plied her with fresh coffee while we waited for the muffins to cool. I mixed a little cream, ricotta and the last of the crushed chocolate to make a topping for the muffins.

She tried to smile some more. "She really said it?"

"She did." I said. "One night in bed. She said it and..."

"And it made a lie of everything." Lex said. "Every Christmas we all had together, every time we ate together, every time she went to your mum or your Nan with the stuff she couldn't talk to anybody else about. Holidays. Stupid little moments that were nothing, but meant everything. They all meant nothing? Because those are family." Lex refused to cry. "You know what my dad told me?" She smiled. "When I was little, he said that God was cruel enough to take my mother away while I too small to know her. But kind enough to give me the chance to choose my family, the ones who loved me as much as any brother, any aunt, and as close to a mother as she could get without adopting me. Choosing family is a rare gift." She smiled. "It was true; 'family friend' doesn't just mean our folks knew each other. It means we were so close that calling your mum an Aunt was so true it might as well have been written in our blood." She clenched a fist. "And Jean was part of that. She says your family aren't her family, then..." She closed her eyes. "Then you aren't the only one she decided to divorce are you?"

"She didn't mean it." I said.

"I know." Lex nodded. "I only wish that meaning and hurting were the same." She stared at me. "Why didn't you tell me?"

"Because she only meant to hurt me." I said.

Lex laughed. "Idiot. Why didn't you tell me when you... Had trouble sleeping?"

"Because repeating the words hurt." I said. "And this? This would have made her the bad guy in the divorce. I didn't want there to be bad guys. Or good guys. Or a winner. I wanted us to move on and get on with being happy."

"And are you happy?" She asked.

"I'm on my way to happy." I said.

There was a knock at my door.

"Jack?" Penny called through the door. "Jack, please be there."

"Penny." I shouted. "Hold on."

"Holy fuck. You didn't make her up." Lex broke into a smile, like the sub breaking through clouds. "Go Birdie."

I smiled and quickened my pace towards the door.

For the few seconds, the tens of steps, between the kitchen and the front door, I was well on my way towards happy.

EIGHT

Penny stood in the doorway and tried to smile, to look as bright as sunshine, as though she did not have a livid bruise across her cheek, a split lip, gravel rash on the hand she was trying to hide. She looked at me, carrying herself at the wrong angle, nursing one side.

"Don't say it." She whispered. "It was nothing."

I stepped back and let her in. Penny started, staring at the woman in my kitchen.

"Lex, this is Penny." I said. "Penny, Lex is a doctor and one of my best friends."

"I've been looking out for Birdie since he managed to beat himself up recently too." Lex said.

"Yeah." Penny nodded. "His side." She looked suspicious. Her every muscle was tightening up, knotting with fear and anger. She gave me a look like she had been betrayed. "Just a friend?"

"I'm not 'just' anything." Lex said. "I'm his good friend."

I gave Penny some coffee, spooned some topping onto a muffin. I placed them all before Penny. She winced as she sat, positioning herself so one foot remained straight. I looked at the way she was carrying herself in a daze.

"What happened?" I asked.

"Nothing." Penny said, glancing at Lex. She flushed, realising nobody was convinced. She rubbed her head. "I had an argument at home. This morning I walked out to clear my head and I had a fall down some steps." She closed her eyes. "I know what you are thinking Jack, but Uncle Bob isn't like that. He didn't hit me."

"Your uncle?" I said. "The thing I'm not meant to ask about."

She nodded. "I couldn't go home. I could not face it yet. Still got those dressings you were buying? Please?"

Lex swore under her breath. "Penny. Jack has a bathroom with a shower. When you have eaten and drunk your coffee, when you are ready, we'll get you upstairs. If you shower, I can take a look a look at you. See if we need to get you to hospital or not. Sound good?"

Penny looked at me for a while.

"We can't ignore this." I said. "Whatever it was when I met you, this crossed a line."

"I'm sorry." She whispered again. "I don't know where else to be."

I stooped down, let her guide my hands to where she had no bruises, cuts, or gravel rash, and let her lean on me a little. "I don't want you anywhere else. You are safe here."

Penny ate her muffin slow. Savouring it. She sipped her coffee and she kept trying to smile as she stared at me. She looked back to Lex and was met by a bright grin. When Penny looked away again Lex gave me a smile, her lips forming a silent 'ooh', of approval. When it came to help Penny up the stairs I let her lean on me. I put an arm around her back and we took it slow. One step at a time. She paused as we passed my bedroom, staring through the open door.

"You okay?" I asked.

"Just dreaming." She whispered, as I let her lean on me again. She looked to the paintings over my bed. "I like those."

"Me too." I said.

I let her get into the bathroom, and Lex took over, closing the door behind her. I could hear there was low muttering chatter beyond the door. I walked away before I heard anything I shouldn't. I walked down to my office in the cellar and closed the door behind me. I dug around in my desk for a leaflet. I had a pupil come to me with problems sometimes. One of them ended up going to a shelter for a while. I found the number I had and rung the manager with some questions.

Just in case.

There was a knock on the door. Penny, looking at me. Her face all full of worries.

"Feeling better?" I asked.

She nodded. "Yeah. Better, but stupid. I left in too much of a hurry. I left my phone, my money, my cards, everything." She closed her eyes. "I have to go back. Sorry."

"No you don't." I held out my hand. "I can go."

"No." She shook her head. "No. If he finds you in there..."

"Then I will explain you asked me to pick some stuff up. I'll be reasonable." I said.

"No." She looked at me. "I have to go."

"Nothing is worth the risk. Surely?" I said quietly. "We can cancel your cards, and your phone can be replaced. But you can't be replaced."

"I left my locket." She whispered. "The only picture of me and my mother. Without him."

"Then you don't have to go alone." I said.

She shuddered. "You don't want to see my house."

"I want you out of there. I want you safe. Here, or at a hostel or..."

"Here?" She smiled, cheeky and full of ideas. "Like..."

I shook my head. "Spare room only. I won't expect a thing in return."

She nodded. The smile still there, but a look of relief in her eyes. "Come with me?"

I smiled. "Of course I will."

*

I parked outside her house. In the daylight it looked a little different. I could see the patches of grey on the woodwork that had once been gloss white. The front garden had nettles and weeds. The windows were dark, the paint on the front door cracked and peeling. The gutter overflowed, and the stains it left on the bricks were sickly brown.

We approached the house together. Penny opened the door and listened carefully before she stepped into the musky air. The textured wallpaper of the hallway had been repainted so many times the pattern of ridges and dots were almost lost. The air felt as thick as soup, damp too. I doubted the windows on the ground floor had ever been opened. There was a living room, with a sofa and a chair pointed at a television, a compact kitchen, the washing machine and the kettle looked well used, the microwave too, but the only washing up waiting at the sink were mugs.

I followed her up the narrow stairs to the first floor. The bathroom door was open. A towel hung by the shower, a glass on the sink held a single toothbrush. The frosted window was speckled with black mould on one edge. There were two bedrooms. One was full of the boxes. The other was where Penny was headed.

A double bed. Clothes piled on a chair. A shelf of books and DVDs. A laptop left charging on the bed, a phone, a purse, and some other stuff on the bedside table. Penny stuffed the purse in her pocket and picked up the phone. She copied four numbers down onto an envelope then with a reluctant growl she threw the phone back on the bed.

"No." She looked around the bedside table, lifting it away. "No. No. No. He took it. He must have took it." She darted across the hallway to the other bedroom. It would once have been the master room, but it was made claustrophobic by the stacks of boxes. She started lifting the boxes, struggling against the weight of clothes, of papers, of records and junk. I helped her lift two, both stuffed with photo albums.

I stared into the room.

"You said he was your father." I muttered.

She looked uneasy.

"Why is there only one bed?" I asked.

Before she could answer there was a creak of floorboards. A groan of wood shifting on the stairs. I looked out in the hallway. Nothing. The house settling. I felt my nerves prickle, the uncanny sense of being watched. A door slammed downstairs.

Penny turned around, looking up at the ceiling, holding up a hand to stop me saying anything.

She looked at me, her eyes wide and distraught.

"Close your eyes." I said.

"Jack, I need to-"

"Close your eyes." I whispered.

She closed her eyes.

"Tell me what the picture in the locket looks like." I said.

"It is me and Mum. At the hospital when I was little. Dad took the picture. He always had cameras at the hospital. All kinds of cameras. It is us, by the rosebush, smiling. Happy. It was a time we were both so happy." She said.

"Okay." I reached over to the boxes of photo albums. "A girl, a woman, a rosebush."

I flicked open the album at the top. It was full of pictures of people in a hospital ward, the equipment, decorations and fashions of their pyjamas all decades out of date. The fifties? Earlier? The pencil notes were unsure. They just said: "The Ward. In Use."

"Those aren't family snaps. They are my father's work."
She said. "Uncle made me bring them all here. They are his
entire life I guess." She looked. "The picture in the locket wasn't
his. Ever. It was Dad." Her shoulders slumped. "I can live
without it. If I ever want to see it you can help me remember."
She kissed my cheek, then stuffed clothes, books, and some
other stuff into a rucksack.

I followed her out of the house. She slammed the door
behind her, double locked the door and dropped her key through
the letter box. "I'm gone now." She shouted at the door. "Gone.
Don't find me. Don't chase me. Leave me alone."

It might have been my imagination, but I was sure the net
curtain for the bedroom twitched. I looked at Penny as she
forced herself to walk away from the house. She got in the car
and said nothing.

"Why was there only one bed?" I asked.

She closed her eyes. "You would not understand."

I put a hand on her knee. "You must be so strong."

She shook her head. "I've lived with him since I was
seventeen. Since I left school. If I was stronger..." She breathed
out. "Can we go anywhere else? Anywhere else at all?"

*

We went to the farmers market. I got a butcher to take a leg of lamb off the bone and roll it. I picked out some vegetables. I had some dried rice in a cupboard and a plan forming in my mind. Penny stayed by my side the whole time. She was trying to lose herself in the crowd, but was looking around, warily.

I felt my stomach knot. It was no way for anybody to live.

She caught my eye, so I gave her a confident smile.

Fuckwit Freak.

The words hit me like a sledgehammer.

I spun on my heels, watching the sea of faces. Trying to work out who might have been close enough to have hissed it in my ear. None of the shoppers flowing through the afternoon seemed to be close enough to have whispered it.

"You okay?" Penny asked.

I nodded mutely, remembering what it was she had shouted at me once when we were kids, and I worked at the cinema to fund my A-Levels. The memory seemed to come from nowhere. I buried it and gave her a confident look. I paid for the vegetables and I ushered her away, looking back the whole time.

*

I was chopping the onions, tomatoes, peppers, carrots and courgettes for the meal. They would make the base on which the lamb roasted. When the meat rested I would add a dash of wine, some stock, and some rice. By the time it was ready to serve the whole meal would be in the dish. For now it was just a growing pile of ingredients. Penny was at the other end of the table with Lex and a bottle of wine that was a little emptier than it should have been. Lex was showing her the Fools Journey with one of my mass produced decks. The major arcana lay in a neat grid, and the suits were stacked up in neat piles.

"Don't worry." Lex said. "He will be careful."

"How do you chop like that?" Penny asked, miming my rapid strokes of the chef's knife.

"With a sharp knife and a lot of-"

"Plasters." Lex finished for me with a wicked smile.

"Practise." I countered.

"And plasters." Lex confided in a stage whisper.

Penny giggled.

"Want me to show you?" I asked.

"Don't." Lex put a hand on Penny to keep her sitting. "He just wants an excuse to stand behind you. Head on your shoulder. Hands on your hands. It's a terrible ploy."

"He ever try it with you?" Penny asked.

"He is in the room." I reminded them.

"Once." Lex shook her head. "Long time ago. Long, long, long, long, time ago."

"Before the divorce?" Penny asked.

"Before the marriage." Lex laughed. "Way back when."

"And?" Penny looked at me. "What went wrong?"

"We were kids in sixth form." Lex gave me an apology with her eyes. "I love the guy, but did you ever see him as a kid?"

"Yeah. I..." Penny looked sick. "I was not very nice about how he looked back then."

"Really?" Lex looked at her. "You, me and a lot of people." She looked suspicious. "How 'not very nice' were you?"

"It doesn't matter." I said. "It was kids, being stupid, it wasn't meant."

"What wasn't meant?" Lex had an insistent tone.

Fuckwit Freak.

I told myself it was a memory. Faded until the scream was little more than a whisper. I dropped the knife to the butcher block and steadied myself.

"You okay?" Lex was clicking her fingers.

"Sorry." I smiled. "I was... I thought I heard something?" I sighed. "Stress. Just stress. Things are... Intense."

Penny looked unconvinced. "I brought my trouble with me. Now it's messing with you."

"Trouble found me long before you did." I gave her my most earnest look. "I fell apart quite badly when the divorce hit home. I think maybe I'm falling apart again a little bit."

"No." She shifted, uncomfortably. "I told you before that I was bad news."

I nodded. "And I told you before I would do whatever I could to help."

I was all too aware of the look Lex was giving me.

"If we can't look after you, we will put you in the direction of a hostel, or a shelter. A refuge. Between us, me and Birdie will find you something." Lex promised firmly. "But for tonight you are safe, and we will have food, wine, friends. All you need to feel at home."

Penny brought the mischief back to her eyes. "Yeah. I do."

"Want to learn to chop like a pro?" I asked.

Penny hesitated and shook her head.

*

After dinner she curled up to me in the lounge. She let me put my arm around her, our bodies entangling. The television was on, but she kept staring at my painting of the cards.

"You know what chills me the most now I see the secret of the King and Queen of hearts?" Penny asked, in a whisper. "Look at their faces. They both love each other. It doesn't matter if he is stabbing himself, or she is stabbing him in the back, they truly love each other."

"We are only truly hurt by the ones we love." I said. "If they mean it or not. If they know what they are doing or not, we care too much about their words. If we didn't care, we wouldn't spare it a second thought. It takes a lot of love to hate."

She smiled. "I think you are right." She kissed my cheek. "Too right."

"I made the bed for you." I said. "My room. I'm going to camp down here."

"I can sleep on a sofa." She said.

"But you don't have to." I said.

"I don't have to go upstairs just yet either." She giggled and curled against me, as much as she could given her pocks of cuts and grazes. She put her head on my chest and we talked.

We didn't need any more. Not right then.

NINE

I wasn't meant to hear it.

In the night floorboards upstairs woke me. I curled up as small as I could on the sofa, the blankets pulled over me, my head buried into the pillows.

I didn't want to hear, but the words were drifting down the stairs through a door that was ajar.

"What do I do?" Penny sounded like she was in tears.

"You go to the shelter." Lex said, gently. "And be safe."

"But..." Penny mumbled something I thankfully could not hear. "I like how he makes me feel. I like that he doesn't act like I'm broken, or nasty, or worthless. And when he is with me, I almost get to believe I'm the person he treats me like." She paused. "I don't want to lose that."

"But you will." Lex said. "Either by walking away now, or by hanging around long enough that he is just worn thin and hollowed out. He's been in a bad place. He'll end up back there. He'll do whatever he can for you, he will try to make you feel that way all the time and deny the shit storm filling the air around him. But... But every day he will carry a drop more guilt. Guilt that he didn't let you do. That he was too scared to break your heart. That he let you fight and fight and fight to keep this working when you could have been happier. Safer...."

"I guessed once he would rather his wife was happy than with him." Penny said.

"He would rather you were safe than with him." Lex said. "When it cuts to the bone, he will do anything for you to be happy and safe. Even say goodbye. And me?" Her tone hardened. "I saw him throw himself to the devil once before for a girl I love like a sister. And I hate what it did for her. I don't know you." She tried to soften her tone. She almost managed it. "I care about him too much to let anybody do that to him again. Even the woman I love as a sister. Understand what I am saying?"

"You sure you don't want me out the way so you can have him?" Penny thought that was funny, which I hoped was just fear and nerves getting to her.

If Lex answered, it wasn't with words.

I rolled back over and promised myself it was a dream, and I hadn't heard a word.

*

At six in the morning I woke with a start as something began to bang upon the front door. A coppers knock, the flat of the hand hammering the door from its hinges. Boom. Boom. Boom.

I zipped up my trousers and walked to the door.

"Who is it?" I demanded, loudly.

"No." Penny was at the top of the stairs. "Don't open the door. Don't let him in." She pulled away the protective arm that Lex had draped over her. Penny was down the steps in a few seconds flat. She pressed herself against the door. "Leave me alone. Just leave me the hell alone."

The door thumped again.

"Listen mate, you can choose to leave, or the police can make the choice for you." I said, trying to sound reasonable. "How about you think about this. For a moment."

"Please." Penny whispered. "Go."

The door stopped banging.

Penny looked at me. Her eyes rimmed with tears. "I can't stay here. It was bad enough thinking he found your number on my phone. But he's following you here." She put her head on my shoulder. "I'm sorry."

"It's okay." I stroked her neck. "Stay here. I'm going to talk to him."

"You can't." She said.

"I want to be sure he's gone." I said quietly. "And maybe..."

"He can't be spoken to." She said. "When he is angry, he can't even think."

I gently pushed her to stay in the house as I opened the door. There was nobody on the drive, or in the front garden. Nobody on the street. The bleak morning would have been empty were it not for the hundreds of photos that were covering the tree. Stabbed on the branches to replace the fallen leafs. I stepped out into the dawn and plucked a few of the photographs down.

Old pictures of the hospital. I was pretty sure they were the ones from the albums in Penny's house. Some were already being stolen by the wind. I walked around to the back garden. There were more photos covering my cherry tree and scattered across the lawn. A tall gangly figure stood among the pieces of paper fluttering in the wind. It was lost in the shadows of the tree.

"Don't do this." I said. "If you care about her, if any part of you loves her, then stop hurting her. Stop thinking you can make her love you. If you have to make her, it isn't love." I held up my hands. "Please. Go."

The figure swept away, through the gate at the back of the garden. I followed it out into the alley, but it was already rounding the corner. I stopped to pick up as many of the photos as I could bundling them up. I looked over my shoulder. Penny was stood at the kitchen sink, staring out the back door, her cheek covered in tears.

Lex appeared behind her, and passed her the leaflet for the hostels. When I went inside I asked Penny what she wanted to do with the photos. She thought long and hard, then told me to burn them. We put them in a deep, metal casserole dish of iron coated in orange enamel. I coated them in vodka and threw a couple matches in there, then let it burn.

"I have to go." Penny said, faintly.

*

It took us two and a half hours to drive up to the M25, then down to the South Coast. We did not talk a whole lot during the drive. Penny scrolled through my MP3 player, looking for songs she liked. She stared out the window. Eventually I parked at a train station. She checked the piece of paper with her instructions written on it.

"It's a few minutes ' walk." She said. "Far enough for you not to know where I'm headed."

I nodded. "You know where to contact me if you need to?"

She gave me the saddest smile she could manage. "You really didn't have to drive me."

"I really did." I said. I hope I sounded like my heart was not shaking itself apart.

"I know..." She closed her eyes. "I know what we had is over before I can call it love." She kissed my cheek, held my hand. "But I adore whatever it was."

I nodded and ran a hand on her side. She moved into the touch, her head tilting. I was about to kiss her, but she stopped me.

"No. Don't. Kiss me now and I want too much. Don't... Don't make me walk away wanting more." She kissed my forehead. "Be careful. Please. You don't know what Uncle Bill is."

"If he comes looking for you I will call the police, I will lawyer up, I will lock the door." I sighed. "I will do whatever it takes to be safe. Don't worry for me."

She put her head on my shoulder, breaking into sobs. "I am so sorry for doing this to you."

She stepped away from the car. She looked back once and then hurried out of the car park and through the street. I sat there, frozen to the steering wheel, letting the music wash over me as I closed my eyes, and rested my head on the window.

It was a long time before I could make myself drive away.

I don't remember anything else until I was parked on my drive. I climbed out the car, unlocked the front door, disarmed the alarm and stepped into the house. I didn't feel anything ominous. There were no creaking floorboards, or whispers on the wind. I half expected an ill omen, but there was nothing. I turned the floodlights on to fill the garden with light. I walked down to the cellar and checked my office. I walked around the ground floor checking the locks on the doors and the windows.

Nothing.

I walked up the stairs. Just to walk between the rooms. I opened the spare room and could smell perfume and sweat. It felt weird for there to be signs of life in the room. It felt warmer. It felt alive. The window was locked. I walked to the bathroom. It was all still. I walked to my bedroom.

The bedsheets were a mess. The smell of Penny clung to them. The smell of her breath, of her hair, and the taste of her skin. I pulled them off the bed and tossed them in the laundry basket. I could not stand the idea of sleeping with her scent haunting my dreams. I could not bear to remember. I shoved them deep into the laundry basket and dumped towels on top of them.

I shoved new sheets, new covers on the bed.

The house was empty. I walked back to the hallway and let out a sigh.

I didn't even have Pickles to talk to.

My phone rang. A withheld number. I had been warned that if Penny wanted to let me know she was safe it would be over a withheld number. I answered and put the phone to my ear. I whipped it away and tried to hang up as I heard the soft scratchy music and vague murmurs.

Where is she?

The words brushed the back of my neck. They sounded ethereal, like they were a memory more than a sound. I looked back behind me as something grabbed me. I only got an impression of a shadow on the wall, of long, narrow, spindle limbs and emaciated flesh hanging from a rib cage. Of deep set eyes and gums drawn back to expose yellowing teeth.

Then I was tipping over the bannister. I fell two meters and met the stairs halfway up their flight. I fell the rest of the way down the wooden hill from Bedfordshire. My head cracked, and my side. One of my arms exploded in pain then I couldn't feel it at all.

I lay on the floor, at the bottom of the stairs.

Give her to me. The words were not made from a voice. They were made from the sounds of branches swaying in the wind and trees bending as they broke. It was a voice made of splinters and tears. Give her to me!

I could not answer. Six fingers were digging into my scalp, slamming my face down to the floor. I felt my nose break. My teeth loosen. A foot hit my ribs so hard I lifted from the floor, then I dropped. I lay still. I lay broken and knotted.

I rolled onto my back. I was alone in the hallway. Yet the front door swung open and the shadows shifted as something stamped down onto my face.

I fell into darkness.

*

"So you didn't see their face?" Detective Reese asked me the question again. He was sat at the side of my hospital bed, his notebook in hand, his phone set to record the interview.

"I didn't have time. My phone rang from the withheld number and..." I felt the words trail off. "And then this happened."

"Okay." Reese nodded. "But you know who it was?"

"His name? No." I shook my head. "But Penny called him Uncle Bob. He lived with her in her house. He had some kind of hold on her."

"Yeah." Reese sighed. "If he lived with her it wasn't legal. Council only had residence for her. They were looking to move her to a smaller residence. While you were out of it her shelter helped her sort the paperwork to give up her claim in town, and start a new claim somewhere else." He looked. "I went there. I saw the crap in that house. My thinking is only one person lived there."

"But you saw all his boxes in her spare room?"

"Yes." He nodded. "I saw other stuff too. And I see that you got a call from a disused switchboard again. They were meant to block the calls, but it only blocked them to your old number. A glitch. The block didn't transfer to your new number."

"It was her Uncle Bob." I said. "He was there when I took her home. She used to hide from his calls."

"And why would she do that if he lived there?" Reese asked.

"Maybe he didn't. But he was at home there. He..." I frowned. "He still controlled her."

"That he did." The detective looked sad. "She... She can't bring herself to tell us much at all. Right now she is in a state that doctors are looking after her too."

I nodded.

"But if this guy exists. He is..." Reese whistled and mimed with his hands. "He's a ghost."

"Jesus." Lex whispered, from the other side of the bed.

"Trouble is, he may think you know how to reach his girl." Reese said. "So we really need to talk about what to do when you get out of here."

"He's living with me." Lex said. She saw the look the detective gave her. "I helped her too. I figure there is safety in numbers. And my house is pretty secure." She paused. "So this same guy was doing the nuisance calls?"

"Picked up Penny's phone. Got the number. Did the hacker magic to make it look like the calls were coming from Bramling Bay, and all when you and Penny met. We checked other calls from the defunct exchange. Asked if they had weird calls. They had. Asked if they met a nice girl from the internet, for coffee, or a film, or whatever else she did on her way to finding you. Casual dates that all went nowhere. Nice, but no spark. Or she rang back to say thanks but no thanks to a second date. You know how it gets. Guess what? They had. All twelve knew her."

"Bramling Bay?" Lex asked.

Reese nodded. "A defunct exchange. Physically gone, but somebody is toying with the records I guess. Jiggering the computers."

"So the guy isn't just acting like a ghost? He wants to be a ghost?" She gave a defiant laugh. "Oh. Great. Bloody great."

"What's the joke?" Reese asked.

"Bramling Bay was a joke." Lex said. "It was Woo-Wooers all dressed up as science, trying to tell the world that they were doing real science. They did just enough to dress their work as science to get a few headlines, but it was a shambles. It was a stunt, not an experiment, and it... It claimed it was an experiment to see if contact could be made with a spirit under certain conditions. It was meant to prove that the effects of the spirit world, or psychic contact, or whatever you want to call it, could be duplicated. So there was this set up in a spooky location, an old hospital and seances dressed as controlled readings, and the psychics were not just told to make contact, but were encouraged to believe anything and everything was contact. We just saw a bit of dust make an orb on the lens? A ghost! Somebody thought they kinda heard something in the dimmed light? Contact! I mean they had pressure after pressure built up until it was a self-fulfilling prophecy."

She stopped.

"Then it all fell to pieces." She said. "You isolate people. You put them in this controlled environment for long enough and control everything they hear, see, think, and you make every conversation they have a feedback loop? If you recruit a whole load of people looking to find a foregone conclusion, and you can convince them of anything. I mean, most the psychics already believed they had powers. This was just proof they thought they could show the world."

"And Bramling Bay was the location?" Reese asked.

"Yeah." Lex said. "But ask me how I know the experiment was a dud."

"Other than the ghost?" Reese raised his hands.

Lex laughed. "Well, there were several spirits that were meant to be contacted. Only one was ever a success. It was all the experiment claimed it needed to be proof. But the ghost they contacted was a control. A fiction. They had better results talking to somebody they made from whole cloth than any of the 'real' ghosts."

"So Uncle Bob is playing at being a ghost." I sighed. "Wonderful."

Lex reached onto the bed and held my hand. "Safety in numbers." She promised me. "You will fix up fine Birdie. You can stay with me a while. Until all this blows over. And Penny? She's safe. She's fine. She's doing fine."

Reese nodded. "The hostel thinks she is doing fine. She's a little quiet. But she's making friends. A little at a time."

I nodded. I told myself a few more weeks and she would forget me. Meet some guy. Become his friend at first. Maybe let herself have a few nights out being social. By the time she realised how easily her arm slipped around him, and how good it felt to cuddle him, she wouldn't even remember my name. One night the movie would become a date, would become the perfect morning after, and at no point would she spare me a thought.

I liked to tell myself that. I don't know if I believed it. I guess I just believed Penny would find a way to be happy.

The detective listened to my story one more time, then thanked me for my patience and went on his way. Lex sat there with me. She held my hand, and we talked about anything else. The first few nights she had refused to leave my side. Eventually the nurses convinced her that she needed to go home. That she should stick to visiting hours.

Apparently they do apply to doctors too, if her name is not on my charts.

Night in the wards was not easy to get used to. The bed felt the wrong size and shape. The air was full of the sounds of other people breathing and moving. Trying not to be heard. The shadows and the light were all unfamiliar. Even the air tasted wrong.

I'm sorry.

The words shocked me awake. The last tendrils of a dream were still in my mind. The feel of warm breath and somebody in the other side of the bed lingered. I lay still. Afraid to move. Afraid of the pain it would bring my flesh if I moved. Of the pain it would bring my heart if I looked to my left. To the darkness and the movement in the corner of my eye.

Jack? The finger just out of sight that stroked my cheek did it in the way only Jean had done. I closed my eyes.

"No." I whispered. "You were in surgery hours ago. You are fine."

I only said sorry for what we became. I felt lips brush my cheek. I never said thank you for what we were. She paused. For never giving up on what we should have been.

I don't blame you because he came for me.

I rolled my head. The space between my bed and the next was empty except for the shadows.

"What?" I struggled to breathe. My own breath tasted rancid and hot. "No."

Hush. It was more a sob than a word. I felt a cheek touching mine, her tears welling in my eyes. I am so proud of my sweet, kind, Birdie. Tell Troy... You know what to tell him.

I choked on a scream, as I felt the sudden cold of her absence.

"No. Don't take her. She was no part of this." I had not realised my voice had raised to a furious roar, until the nurses were crowding me. I stopped screaming and lay back in my bed, the worms of guilt feasting on my core.

TEN

"It was murder." Troy said blankly. "No other word for it." He stood over my bed, shaking. He gave me a weak smile. "I thought you had as much right to know as anybody else." He held out his hands. "And don't worry, your alibi is pretty sound."

"Murdered how?" I asked.

"After the surgery, she was still under. I was sitting with her to watch over her. I stepped out to let my family know she got through it, and thought I saw somebody leaving her room. Just a glimpse of somebody tall and thin. I get worried, I head back, and I... I can see the difference. She isn't under. She isn't slow in waking. She has bruises over her mouth, blood around her nose. Somebody pinched her nose shut, clamped her mouth, waited for her to stop bucking. I was on the phone a couple of minutes, and... And..." He looked defeated.

"Not your fault." I said.

"No." He clenched his fist. "Damn I wish I could blame you too. If it is this fucker you invited into your life for some girl to fuck." He forced his fist to unclench. "But no. That isn't fair. Only one to blame is..."

"It happened because of me." I looked away. "I get some of the fault. Some of the responsibility."

Troy refused to listen. "No. The person who did this gets to pay. It won't be you. I saw the CCTV footage. Some skinny guy who looks like he escaped a morgue. He gets to pay."

He looked at me futility burning in his eyes.

Seconds passed in which neither of us had any idea what to say. I don't know what strange dream it was that made Jean appear to me. I can't imagine she would waste her last message on me and not on Troy. But something thought I would know what to say.

"Troy." I looked away from his gaze. "However much you think she loved you, whatever joy and hope and brilliance you think you brought to her life, double it. Double it again. She... She didn't always know how to show anybody how happy she was. She would hide in work rather than open her heart. You think you meant the world to her, but you meant everything. All of life, all of this world and every other. All of creation. Whatever she faced when she went to sleep, she would have known no fear, because her dreams were all waiting for her when she woke up."

He stared at me. "That was one of her poems."

"Published a month after we..." I coughed. "Written when it wouldn't be for me. And that was when she was terrified. Imagine what all that became when she knew it was the forever kind of love."

He nodded. He knew I had been clumsy, but he appreciated the effort. He slumped into the chair and looked like his soul had been ripped out of him, leaving a cold, dark, void where his heart should have been.

"This other girl." He said. "If the monster who did this is looking for her, he can't have her. Nobody else gets hurt for whatever the hell this is."

I nodded.

"Who is he Birdie?"

"I don't know." I said. "Far as I can tell he is a pile of boxes and old photogra-" I stopped. "Old photographs. He phoned me from numbers that belonged to an old hospital that some kind of experiment was run in. He wants to be a ghost. He had all these photographs of a hospital. The same hospital. And..." I felt something click. "And even Penny's locket was a photograph of a hospital. I bet all those photos and all those boxes were to do with the experiment."

"Sounds like an obsession." Troy looked thoughtful. He had something to throw himself behind so he didn't have time to feel the grief. "Obsessions can be useful. If he got hold of papers from an experiment we can find out where. Somebody ran the experiment. Somebody will know who sold the materials. Who bought them."

"They are in Penny's house. All boxed up." I said.

"Then I need to speak to the police. Tell them that maybe we can help them find something in those boxes." He dug out a phone. "You up to trying?"

I nodded.

I didn't have any way out of the mess. I figured I needed to see it through.

*

A few days later when I was let out of hospital wrapped up like a mummy under my clothes, with my face mottled purple and brown by bruises, I was stood by poky little house in the estate with the bad reputation. The door was still cracked and peeling. The shadows still dark and dank. The air had not got any fresher.

"Shall we?" Reese asked, digging the key (borrowed from the landlord) from his pocket. He was a burly man, with a friendly, piggy face, sandy hair turning white with age. He was at the point that he was counting the days instead of the months to retirement.

He pushed the door open.

I walked for the stairs, pausing and listening before I reached the top. I forced myself to go on. As I reached the top of the stairs Reese looked around to ensure there were no murderers hiding. I opened the spare room. A few of the photo albums were laying empty, but there were a whole lot more that were still stuffed full. I flicked them open.

"Bramling Bay?" Troy asked, showing me one of the books of photographs of a hospital in the war. He flicked through a few pages of photographs to find one of two nurses standing by the sign. He tapped the photograph. "These must be from the experiment."

I lifted the boxes of albums out the way and revealed a box papers. I lifted them out and started to put them in order. "Enquiry Society for the Preternatural." I read from the title pages. "Loom Experiments."

He took one of the documents from me and started reading it. "So not a University?"

"In a way. A student group. With about as much standing as their Monty Python appreciation association." I scratched my hair and sat down, found one of the overviews and started to read.

"So, where would they have bought these?" Reese asked.

"The group is gone, so one of the members?" Troy guessed. "We can start with the ones still at the University." He was surfing the internet on his phone.

"Penny was too young to be one of the volunteers. But her mum?" I smiled as I found a page in the document that listed the supposed psychics, mediums, and other 'sensitive' volunteers. "Her mum was a medium who volunteered. Hence her locket being a photo of them at the hospital." I paused. "The last without him."

"What?" Reese stared at me.

"She lost a locket. She said it was the last picture of her and her mum without Him." I could feel something in my thoughts, just out of reach, just out of focus. I looked back to the boxes of photo albums and started opening them one at a time. A lot were photos of the hospital from all through its history. Then suddenly there were family albums. I opened them and flicked through pages of Christmases and awkward holiday snaps. Then... Then I started to see it.

It wasn't even Penny's family. I think it was one of the other volunteers. The rest of the pictures were still of Christmases, Christenings, and family gatherings, but they all had the same blemish. Lurking behind the crowds, like a stain in the matte of the photographs was a tall, thin smear. A distortion, a blur, a haze. If you squinted you could almost believe it was another figure standing in the crowd. You might convince yourself you could see elongated limbs, and an emaciated form. The hint of a skull on a long neck.

I dropped it and looked at the next album. It was Penny's family. Around her ninth birthday party the skeletal blur started to lurk in her photographs. It started looming behind her father, leaning over her mother, draping one hand over the shoulder of a troubled little girl.

"What are those?" Troy asked.

I shook my head and chose another of the boxes. Hand written note books. An identity card for the university, decades old was used as a bookmark in one of them.

"Does Doctor Moran still work at the University?" I asked, imagining the fresh faced young doctor with another couple of decades on his waistband, some hair silvered and retracting. I looked deeper. There was a locket at the bottom of the box. I lifted it out and saw a picture of a young and toothy Penny beaming back.

"Yeah." Troy said.

I showed him the card. "Want to go have a word?"

"Oh yeah." Reese moaned. "Leave me to take care of all this evidence." He rolled his eyes and reached for a phone. "Well, I need to get some people to start looking at all this. The Met are going to love my bulking out their murder investigation."

"I don't suppose I can take some of this?" I said.

Reese narrowed his eyes. "Evidence."

I held up my hands. "Okay. Sorry." I took some pictures on my phone instead. He seemed to have less of a problem with that. "I'm going to see if Lex is available."

Troy nodded. He held up a hand. "Hello. Yes. Moran please. Oh he won't know me, my name is Troy Johan. I'm researching Project Loom. Or the Loom Experiments. I need to see him urgently about-" He looked at me.

"Just tell him 'Penny'. He will know without the surname."
I said.

"Penny and her Uncle Bob." Troy said. "Could you be
careful to use those exact words in your message. Now, my
numbers..."

As I stepped out of the house I paused and looked around.
I looked for a tall thin shadow lurking somewhere. I saw none.
But I had the uncanny feeling of being watched. It was only then
that I realised the locket was still in my hand. I let it drop from
the chain and held it up, looking at the way it spun and sparkled
in the sunlight.

Troy stood behind me. "So do we wait for an appointment,
or do we risk going to look for this Moran guy ourselves?"

I flicked out my phone and dialled for Lex.

*

Professor Moran was a little taller than me, with narrow
features, hair clipped short to disguise a receding hairline, a little
grey at the temples, a neat beard, and a voice that was trying
too hard to sound middle class. He was a little too well bred for
his turns of phrase, trying to sound like the spoon he was born
with was only silver plated. He emphasised his home counties
accent a little too strongly.

He sat on one side of a desk covered in paperwork. Myself,
Troy and Lex were on the other.

"What is your interest in the case?" Moran smiled knowingly as he stirred his coffee. "Because funny story. I have two police forces asking questions."

"I'm the subject of the Kent Constabulary investigation." I said. "I was beaten up by somebody claiming to be a ghost. A ghost who never was."

"Oh, now I wouldn't say that." Moran almost laughed. Almost. "Uncle Bob may not have the ghost of a dead person, but for all intents and purposes he was real. The experiences we produced were real. The interactions were real. He took on a life of his own, so to speak, that was not contained by our little experiment."

"Because he was answers on a ouija board?" I shook my head. "The ghost in the ideomotor machine?"

"We know how ouija boards work." Lex said.

"But he was bigger than a board. Making the glass move may be a trick, but the answers? The personality the subjects described? The questionnaires? The sightings?" He waved for us to sit down. "We had twelve people in three groups of four holding sessions of various kinds to contact the ghosts. For three of the spirits, we had mixed results. Two groups made contact with one, but the personality of the ghost differed between the two groups. The other only one gave potential results that were inconclusive. But Bob? All three groups made contact. We had given some very basic information packs to all the groups on all the ghosts. Enough that for the real spirits, the ones people reported seeing all through the life of the hospital, the groups could make contact, then ask set questions. Some could be checked for historical accuracy, some were unknowns that could not be researched before hand. The idea was that the unknowns would be identical in all groups if we made serious contact."

"And in Bob's fictional case?"

"I left some breadcrumbs. If people were cheating they would use the false facts I dropped around. And some unknowns. Now here is where it gets interesting. They went through the standard questions in their various ways of making contact. They all got the wrong answers for the 'knowns', but they got the same wrong answers. For the 'unknowns' their answers were... varied but close. Enough to be differences in interpretation." Moran looked proud. "I know, some of the questions were leading, but even so. How they went off script was... Amazing."

"And then?" Troy asked.

"And then they started to see him. They described the same person. Tall. Gaunt. Corpse like. Six fingered on one hand." He looked upset. "Around the same time they began to feel wary. Groups reported he was turning uneasy. Angry. In constant pain. It was tragic really. And..."

"And?" Lex sounded cold.

"And always asking about the girl." Moran admitted.

"This girl?" I dropped the locket in my hand.

"He..." Moran looked around. "He asked about a lot of people. But everybody liked Pen. We wanted to protect her. Her mum had trouble getting a sitter. Sometimes she had to bring Penny to sessions. She was never part of the session, but she did seem to report being aware of the ghost a lot. Just as much as the readers and guides in the groups."

"And when the experiment ended?" I asked.

"If you read anything about it you would know. For several years we collected photos from the subjects that contained an anomaly. Evidence of a ghost. A being summoned from the ether who could interact with the subjects. All reported small items going missing. Things going bump in the night. Messages. And..." He smiled. "When she turned twenty two Penny got in touch. She said she wanted to honour her mum's memory by writing a memoir. A record of their story. Of Bob. We needed to clear out the materials. I gave her what I could to help."

"Penny bought it all?" I asked.

"Penny and other members of the group. Most weren't young when we started. The herd has thinned. Penny is the last one still looking into it. As far as I know." He shifted.

"What aren't you telling me?" I demanded.

"Nothing." He met my eyes. "Nothing." He promised.

"You wanted rid of the materials." I said. "You were... Relieved?"

He shook his head. "I... I admit I was glad that certain things stopped bothering me quite so often once I gave her the materials." Moran looked ashamed. "I was happy to shift the monkey from my back to hers. There was only so many times I could stand to be pushed down stairs or to wake up with bruises. That thing... As beautiful as it was, it was disturbed. Troubled. But kind. Sweet. It cared greatly for the child. For the women. It could not help the pain in it's past."

"Over ten years." I said. "Over ten years ago she wanted to right a book on her mum and her ghostly adventures. And since then it has been with her. Holding her under it's thumb. Like an abusive lover. Demanding to know where she was. Hurting her. Harassing her. Calling her. She had to hide from it at night where it could not call her."

"We gave life to something." Moran said darkly. "It only exists as much as we believe in it, and she knew it was real. It was more real to her than anybody else. As a child, it was this tragic, pained figure, but kind and sweet and funny too. She loved it. And it loved her. Perhaps when she collected the materials she began to believe in it again?" He shook his head. "Or perhaps it saw she did not believe in it at all. Perhaps it is fighting to survive."

"Or perhaps it just likes hurting people." Troy said. "Or perhaps, some sick son of a bitch wants it alive so much they are willing to make it real. To kill in the name of a delusion."

"It is real." Moran snapped. "That delusion would bite me. It would kick me and punch me. When it thought I was forgetting it. When I was leaving the project on a shelf to rot and die. When I refused others the chance to make documentaries, it went wild at me."

"So why let Penny write about it?" Lex asked.

"Because... If you are in a crowd and you see a lion chasing you, you do not have to outrun the lion." Moran smirked. "I tried to be brave. I tried to defy Uncle Bob and let him die. I got kicked and thrown from my bed. Haunted. So I let Penny take it away. Now she is gone, and there is a lion out there. So my running shoes are on, and you, poor sods one and all, have a fucking limp."

"Wonderful." I sighed.

"Except this is bull." Lex said. "This is all bull."

"Oh yes. See how convinced he is by that." Moran sniffed.

"How do I stop it?" I asked.

"You don't." Moran laughed. "You let it find Penny and you sigh with relief."

I shook my head. "No. I don't. How do I stop it?"

"How do you lay to rest a man who never lived?" Moran scoffed. "Don't be absurd."

I looked at him. "Somebody is using your toy ghost to hurt people. To kill."

"Yes." Moran nodded. "Uncle Bob is. Cleansings did not work. Exorcisms did not work. All you can do is give him what he wants, and what he wants is Penny."

I sat there. I stared at him.

"Then I find something he wants more." I rubbed my head.

If he loved Penny, if he truly loved Penny, there was only one thing I could offer him.

ELEVEN

We sat in the car. Music played and rain fell, while Troy drove. I was on the back seat. Lex sat in the front, but kept looking over her shoulder at me. Lex was looking at my phone, at the pictures I took of the documents. Of the pictures I took of old photograph albums. She zoomed in, to look at the shadow on the background of a few of them. She was frowning intently.

"Well this is interesting." She said. "But we didn't happen to snap pictures of Penny, so we don't know if whatever this is, is what beat the crap out of you. Or.. Or... You know..." She looked at me. "But the way I see it. Either somebody is trying to be this ghost to make lives hell. Or perhaps some of the stuff you experienced wasn't stress, painkillers, and tricks of the mind. But either way, if they want to be the ghost the only way to make contact is to reach out to the ghost, right?"

I nodded. "So. I go buy a bell, a candle, and a bible. Then I get my Masterpiece Deck and..."

"And in ten to twelve years I get parole." Troy muttered.

"You don't want to do that." Lex said.

"He took Jean from me." Troy said. "If he wants to be a ghost this bad, I will make his wish come true. If he already is a ghost..." He shrugged.

"Jesus." Lex shook her head. "When did my life get so messed up?"

"Year five. You joined the school, sat next to me, and did not listen to girls telling you not to talk to the freak, as you would just encourage me." I said.

"Yeah." Lex nodded. "Good job I love you Birdie, or I would slap you back to hospital for this." She locked eyes with me for a second. Her smile thinned out, became embarrassed.

The car fell into silence.

*

I sat in my living room, surrounded by candles. The lights were low. Lex had found some suitable mood music on her MP3, and it was playing softly from the stereo. Troy was pacing around looking anxious. He watched me shuffling the cards. He sipped his coffee.

"Want to take a seat?" I didn't look up from the cards. "Choose wisely, left hand of me, or right hand of me?"

He stared at me. "For real?"

"You want the ghost to think we are taking this seriously, sit to his right." Lex said.

"Why?" Troy took the seat anyway.

"Because when you speak, the ghost will want to listen to a right hand man. You have authority." Lex sat on my left. "And I will have influence." She put a hand on my thigh. "You really ready to do this?"

"I'm ready. I'm just not sure how to know if Bobby-Boo is ready to play." I said.

Proud of you. All of you.

"I know." I whispered.

"What?" Troy said.

There was a pounding on the door. A firm, flat handed, thump upon the door, making it shake against the hinges. One. Two. Three.

"I don't think you need me to open the door." I shouted.

The flames on the candles flickered and danced. I lifted the small bell and rang it. It tinkled and jingled. I set it on the table. I set the bible beside it.

The air grew still. Just us and the music. The kind of stillness that made it hard to draw breath. That made it hard to make a sound. We were frozen, listening, waiting for the creaking floorboard that groaned in the hallway.

"This isn't an exorcism." I said. "This is a conversation. You want to talk, then there is a little bell here. All you need to do is ring the bell, or give us a sign.

Fuckwit-Freak.

The words hissed past my neck.

I could see the others flinching, wondering if they heard something. There was a noise in the kitchen. A cacophony of dull thuds and thumps. I stood and walked to the door, in the kitchen, my butchers block was covered in a forest of knives. All my sharpest kitchen knives were rammed tip first into the wood. They were wobbling side to side.

"Well." Troy sighed. "That is a sign."

"And this is officially in the unknown and shit scary territory." Lex said, pointing her camera at the knives. She looked at me. "Birdie?"

I sat back at the table. I shuffled the major arcana. "Ok. Let's see who I am talking to."

I dealt seven cards face down.

The light bulb overhead flickered and died. The music stuttered to a halt. The air grew frigid. The shadows darker. The sound of our own breathing seemed to find an echo from nowhere.

Do you want to know who I lay awake and think about?

"Memories already hurt me." I said. "They lose their sting after a while. Let's talk with your voice. Not Penny. Not Jean. You." I stared into the shadows. I could feel the darkness around me. "You managed to speak before."

The bell flew from the table. It bounced across the floor.

"Okay." I said, turning over the first card as Troy and Lex stood behind me. "How about for now I do some of the talking?"

"Your head is the chariot." I said. "Control, assertion, domination. Perhaps once you were trying to be a guiding, caring influence, but it's all changed now isn't it?"

I closed my eyes. I could feel him across the table from me. Breathing hard and ragged, settling in the chair so that it groaned against the wooden floor. I could feel the taint of cold he painted the air with. I could taste the grave and the dank.

I opened my eyes to look at the empty chair. I flipped over the left hand pair. The World inverted. The woman in the circle and surrounded by the animals was upside down. Next to her was Judgement, also upside down. Also inflected. "The World inverted. You have a purpose for which there is no completion, no closure, no end. It is all the wrong kind of eternal isn't it. You just can't move on. You just can't let go."

I stared at the chair. The shadows were as thick as oil. The darkness clung to the chair. It stared back at me with pale eyes as it started to take form. Lex was whispering a prayer under her breath I had not heard since her father passed.

Troy was staring, resolute, angry. His fists were clenched.

I turned over the heart cards. The Lovers. The Emperor reversed. "So many cards that were once the right way up are turning around for you aren't they? The Lovers. You love Penny. Perhaps you love all those you watched over for so long. Who you spoke to. Who you followed home. But they all let you go. They all faded away eventually. All except one. And you will do anything to hold on to her. The Emperor used to mean that you were a father figure, a brother, a guide. The solid foundation of her life. But now he turns his back on you. Domination, control, strings and chains. Not a healthy thing to-"

I was thrown from my chair. I slammed to the wall as six sharp fingers closed around my throat. I stared at the naked man who held me aloft. Who squeezed my throat until air could not fill my lungs. His eyes were wild, his skin pale, his skeletal form jagged and sharp beneath the shroud of leathery flesh. His yellow teeth in a grimace. Cold washed over me. What little breath I could draw was a silver mist.

"Go on." I whispered. "Prove I'm right. Kill me."

He bounced my head off the wall.

"And what then?" Lex snapped with absolute authority in her voice. "Penny welcomes you in open arms? She leaps at the chance to be with the person who killed her friend?"

Not. Friend.

Troy stepped forwards and punched the thing three times. None of them made the slightest difference. He might as well have been punching a statue. Uncle Bob turned to look at Troy.

Stop.

The word came from the ghost, but it was Jean's voice. Her word. Screamed and angry.

Stop. Stop saying that. Stop saying that!

"Bastard." Troy looked like he had been hit in the chest. His wind knocked out of him. "Bastard." He hammered the ghost with his fists. Bob dropped me so he could turn on Troy, hurling the younger man into my book case. He slammed it to the wall, and Troy fell to the floor, curling into a protective ball.

Uncle Bob had become smoke and shadow, lost in the flickering candle light.

"Do you think that works?" Lex shouted to the shadows, turning on her heel to look in all directions as she stood over Troy. "Do you think Penny wants a killer? Of are you going to force her to be with you? Is she somebody you love, or who you beat to your will?"

I walked back to the table, and turned over the right hand cards. The Devil dancing with Death.

"This is what you give to the world." I said. "Death and the Devil dancing together."

There was a roar.

"This is all you can offer Penny." I said.

I was answered by a whirlwind. A sudden gust that drove the cards and the paper to the air. It whipped the whole room to a frenzy of howling gales and chaos. Bob was stood on the table, his talon like toes scratching grooves in the walnut. His fingers tight around the grip of a knife held high over his head.

"No!" Lex screamed the word. She was trying to pull me aside.

"Lex. Get out." I said as calmly as I could, staring into the eyes of the six fingered fiend. At the despair and the turmoil there. "Troy. Go. Go now."

Troy grabbed her. He wrapped his arms around her and tossed her towards the door. He shoved her shoulders to push her out of the room.

"No." Lex snarled. "What are you doing you idiot?"

"Offering him something better." Troy said quietly.

No.

The ghost howled in Lex's voice.

If I want to vomit I'll let you touch me.

We were kids, and she was my world, and in my defence, I really was teaching her to chop onions with style. I did ask if she would mind me stepping closer.

I tried to smile at the memory.

"You can do this." I said. "Or you can love her enough to let her be happy. To let her be safe. To..."

Hurts.

No voice for that one. Just splintering wood and breaking stones.

"I know." I said. "Even without the bruises."

HURTS.

"You want to love somebody, you learn about hurt pretty quickly. You learn how hurt them without intending to. You learn to live with the hurt they didn't mean you. Sometimes you learn to live with the hurt they meant. If you are lucky, what is left is still love." I stared at Bob. "If you have to kill me to finally let go of Penny, then kill me. Do it right this time. At least you will never find her."

IT HURTS

"Then let go." I said. "Just let go. Let her go. Lover her enough to be happy for her. Even if it leaves you hollow. Even if it leaves you empty. It's the only way you have to show them what they me-"

The knife fell to the table. The tip dug into the wood, right in the middle of the scratches. The candles all went out, tendrils of smoke reaching the ceiling from their wicks.

There was silence.

I slumped to a chair. I sucked in breath and tried not to think how I was going to end that sentence. At how the words had been burning my throat. Troy let Lex go and she ran over to me. She knelt beside me and wrapped her arms around me, her head on my shoulder.

"Don't ever do that again." She whispered. "Idiot."

I nodded and held her back. "Troy?"

He shook his head. "It's gone. Isn't it."

I nodded.

"And it was hurting." He looked at his hands, tried to make them into a fist. "Maybe I wanted to hurt it more. But..." He shook his head. "Maybe Jean wouldn't want me to be that man."

"Maybe there isn't much of a maybe about it." Lex said. She stroked my hair back out the way, so she could touch her cheek to mine.

"So what happens now?" I asked.

*

"It's been weeks since I heard anything. Felt anything." Penny said, sipping a beer from a long, tall glass. We were sat in the beer garden of her new local on the kind of hot and hazy summer afternoons we don't get enough of. "Further I travel, the less I feel like he is... You know..."

"I think I do." I looked up at the cloudless sky. I tried to look anywhere but at her.

"I..." She chewed on her words. "I think you have to be part of what I left behind."

I nodded. "I know."

"But I found a job. Some friends. It's working out." She drummed her fingers on the table.

"So why ask to see me now?" I smiled. "Not that I am ungrateful to see you looking like this."

She flushed. "I wanted to do this right. I know it's stupid."

"You met somebody?" I asked.

She smiled. "He was at a shop near the hostel. A coffee place I used to go in. Regular enough that we got chatting. And..."

"And you should ask him out." I said.

She looked at me.

"Okay. Which coffee place? I could do with something full fat with a caramel syrup. I can hint without any kind of subtlety that my friend really likes one of the staff, and maybe he should offer to take her to see the film about robots fighting werewolves." I held up my hands.

"No." She squawked the word and laughed. "Why would you do that?"

"Because if you like him enough to risk this, he is worth making an arse out of myself for." I shrugged. "And because you would be happy."

She gripped my hand. "Okay. I will do the asking. But thanks." She met my gaze. "So do me a favour so I feel we are equal?"

"Okay." I said.

"Ask out Lex."

I laughed. "No. I mean... She wouldn't..."

"She loves you." Penny rolled her eyes. "Not in love with you. But she should be."

"She will say no." I said.

"And she will forget it five minutes later." Penny said. "But if she says yes, she will remember it always. I promise you that." She closed her eyes. "And... And I lost you so much. Both of you. Least I can do is push you towards something a little better. Okay?"

"I don't think that is on the cards." I warned. "She has dates. She never has trouble dating."

"But they aren't you." Penny gave me her wisest look. "See if it is on the cards. You have enough of the buggers. See what you tell yourself with them."

"Just... Just go rock the world of coffee shop guy." I said, with what I hoped was a bright, encouraging smile. She matched it and patted my hand.

We talked more for the afternoon. That evening I went to Lex's. She had a few friends over and we were cooking for them. She let me teach her to chop the vegetables, and didn't complain any about my hands being over her hands. My face next to hers.

So tomorrow I have something I think I should ask her.